GIDEON'S FORCE

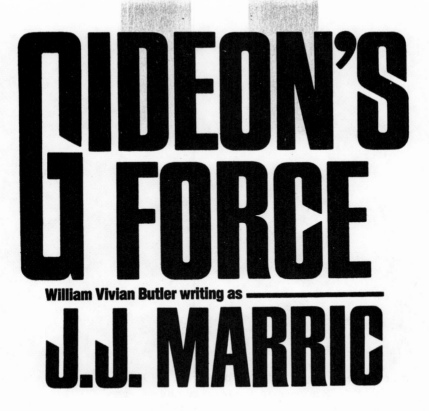

GIDEON'S FORCE

William Vivian Butler writing as

J.J. MARRIC

sD

STEIN AND DAY/*Publishers*/New York

First published in the United States of America in 1985
Copyright © 1978 by the executors of the late John Creasey
All rights reserved, Stein and Day, Incorporated
Designed by Louis A. Ditizio
Printed in the United States of America
STEIN AND DAY/Publishers
Scarborough House
Briarcliff Manor, N.Y. 10510

Library of Congress Cataloging in Publication Data

Butler, William Vivian, 1927-
    Gideon's force.

    I. Creasey, John.   II. Title.
PR6052.U87G5   1985   823'.914   84-40730
ISBN 0-8128-3027-X

For
CAROL

Contents

GIDEON'S FORCE

1

Estate of Fear

GEORGE GIDEON, THE commander of the Criminal Investigation Department at New Scotland Yard (CID), normally breakfasted heartily.

This morning—a hot, sunny Tuesday morning in early September—every mouthful of bacon was an effort to swallow and the accompanying coffee too tasteless to drink without a wry grimace.

It was nothing to do with the cooking. All food and drink is unappetizing to a bone-dry tongue and palate; and the feeling inside him was driving every drop of saliva from his mouth.

It was a complicated feeling. There was anger in it but also frustration, horror, bewilderment, strangeness, shame.

The Law—which he, Gideon, had served, represented, fought for all his working life—was breaking down.

It was happening—of all places—here, virtually on his own doorstep.

And there wasn't a man in England, it seemed, who could begin to tell him why.

About a mile north of Gideon's home—a solid, Victorian house in Harrington Street, Fulham—there was a new residential area called the Wellesley Estate. This Estate, which was about a mile wide by a mile and a half in length, had been built under the auspices of the Greater London Council, primarily to house families from overcrowded London areas; and for an Estate of its type, it wasn't at all bad. Gideon wouldn't have liked to have lived on it himself. There was too much concrete about, too slick a pattern. He would, before long, have yearned for the sight of a single stretch of homely old red brick. But the facilities there were undeniably excellent. The Wellesley Estate was as handsomely equipped as a miniature New Town. It had a complete set of gleaming modern schools—infants, middle and high; a splendid shopping mall with everything from a chiropodist's to a supermarket, and an air-conditioned community center where, ordinarily, churches of many denominations held services on Sunday, bingo was played on Mondays, Wednesdays, and Fridays, and there was a disco every Saturday. The amenities also included three good public houses, a full-size football field, and an adventure playground for the under-twelves.

There were, unquestionably, many worse places in England to live in than the Wellesley Estate.

Why, then, had its inhabitants suddenly gone mad and turned it into a hell of purposeless violence? Why did no day or night go by without its quota of muggings, rapes, assaults—and on two occasions, actual murders? What strange force impelled the orgies of window-smashing and fire-raising that happened there? And above all, why was it that as soon as the police asked questions, they were met by a wall of silence as thick as a slab of Wellesley concrete?

Violence, as such, wasn't unusual in these days. Sporadic outbreaks of brutality and vandalism were occurring all over Britain, and there were many areas—even wealthy residential ones—where a lot of the older and lonelier residents lived in constant dread. But on the Wellesley Estate the situation had gone much further than that. Fear, at a level where it could almost be described as terror, had become an ever-present fact of life for every man, woman, and child. And the horror of the Yard's helplessness to alter the situation had become an ever-present fact of life for Gideon, and one liable to intrude on his mind at any moment and turn that moment into a waking nightmare.

It wasn't that the Yard hadn't acted. It had done so repeatedly. After one night of fire-raising, the Uniform Branch had moved in and virtually lined the main streets of the Estate from end to end. They had stayed on duty, night and day, for a week; the only quiet week the Estate had had in its short history. But there were heavy demands on Uniform's manpower.

"Saturation policing," as the commissioner had called that operation, couldn't be sustained indefinitely, and eventually the Uniformed Force had had to go, to be replaced by patrolling area cars. The cars hadn't proved effective. That same night, the muggers, fire-raisers, and window-smashers had returned.

Gideon's CID had taken over. Under Chief Detective Superintendent Tom Riddell, one of the most aggressively determined men in the Force, a long series of house-to-house searches had been organized; hundreds of people had been detained for questioning; night after night, watches had been maintained from hidden "stakeouts" in the hope of catching the miscreants red-handed. But there seemed to be some kind of intelligence network operating against the police. Tom Riddell's efforts had resulted in pitifully few arrests, and he himself was looking more strained, more haggard, with every passing day—a fact that added to Gideon's worries. He wouldn't enjoy telling Tom that he would have to replace him; but if things went on like this, it would soon be his duty to do so.

Or, *would* it be his duty? Wouldn't he, perhaps, by giving such an order, be making Riddell a scapegoat? Could it be denied that Tom was doing just about everything that could humanly be done?

Humanly. That brought up another consideration. Although his massive bulk and belligerent air belied it, Riddell was essentially a vulnerable human being. A couple of years before, a difficult case—involving Black Power and Rachmanism—had brought him within a hairsbreadth of having a nervous breakdown. Was there a danger that the Wellesley Estate business was driving him the same way?

If so . . .

"Pass the marmalade, dear."

"The what?" Gideon was astonished to find himself starting violently. "Oh, the marmalade. Yes. Yes, of course."

He picked up the pot, and dutifully passed it to his wife, Kate. At the same time, he made a supreme effort to pull himself together. At this rate, it would be he who was not going to pieces.

He sneaked a glance at Kate, hoping that she hadn't noticed how little he'd eaten of his amply cooked breakfast. It was a forlorn hope, as he well knew. Those calm, blue gray eyes of hers—calm, but so keenly observant—didn't miss much where he was concerned. This morning,

13

though, they had a preoccupied look, and Gideon suddenly realized he was in luck. Kate's thoughts were miles away.

He knew well enough what was on her mind. In three weeks' time, after nearly a year of postponement because of the couple's other commitments, their eldest daughter, Penny, was going to be married to Deputy Commander Alec Hobbs, Gideon's right-hand man at the Yard. Penny was insisting on a white wedding, with every imaginable trimming; and Kate was at the center of all the preparations. The fact that Penny—a leading pianist with the BBC Symphony Orchestra—was herself in the middle of a full program of appearances at the promenade concerts in the Royal Albert Hall didn't exactly help. She had given an exhausting solo performance at the proms only the previous night and at the moment was still in bed, sleeping it off.

Remembering these family affairs did Gideon a world of good. The Wellesley Estate question vanished temporarily from his mind with the speed of a bursting bubble. He helped himself to more coffee and drank it less stoically than before.

"Got a lot on today?" he asked.

"That's putting it mildly," Kate replied and suddenly stood up, her tall, slim body moving with the languorous grace that never deserted her, no matter how many years went by. "Lord, is that the time? I ought to give Penny a call."

"Oh, let her sleep," Gideon said. "She deserves it after last night. I managed to catch the tail end of her performance on the car radio—and the applause went on for minutes."

"I only wish I could," Kate said with a sigh, "but Penny's got a pretty full day. Marjorie Beresford, who's doing an alteration to her wedding dress, is coming at half-past eight."

Marjorie Beresford . . . For a moment, Gideon couldn't put the name to a face, the face to a name. Then suddenly, he remembered. Marjorie was the widow of Detective Sergeant Sam Beresford, who had died heroically, tackling three armed bank thieves single-handed in Fulham High Street about five years before. Marjorie had a son, Gideon remembered, a boy of eight at the time of the shooting; he'd be thirteen now. No doubt this dressmaking was her way of eking out her police widow's pension. It was typical of Kate to think of helping someone like that at a time like this.

Kate read his thoughts and frowned.

"Don't think we're employing her out of charity, George. Marjorie took a course at one of the big fashion houses. She really is the best dressmaker for miles. And very much in demand."

Gideon grinned.

"She must be, if it's necessary to knock her customers up at eight thirty A.M. Couldn't she possibly have fixed an afternoon appointment—or an evening one?"

"Certainly not an evening one. No one dreams of being out after dark where Marjorie lives."

Gideon tensed.

"Where *does* she live?"

"She moved last year to Wellington Avenue. You know. On the Wellesley Estate."

Perhaps because she knew what emotive words Wellesley Estate were to him, Kate's voice had become exceptionally calm and matter-of-fact. She made it sound as though it was the most natural thing in the world that there should be certain areas of their own home town where people stayed indoors after dark. But, to Gideon, it was the most diabolically *un*natural thing in the world; a denial, in a sense, of all that Sam Beresford, and dozens of policemen like him, had given their lives for.

The feeling of fury and frustration came back so strongly that it almost choked him. He got up from the breakfast table, gave Kate a peck on the cheek, and walked quickly out of the dining room into the hall.

He turned back at the front door and managed to force a gruff cheerfulness into his voice.

"Congratulate Penny for me on last night's performance. Tell her I'll be sending out for all the papers to read for myself the praise and adulation. Though I've no doubt Alec will be coming in with the whole of Fleet Street under his arm."

Half a minute later, he had driven his car—a large, comfortable Rover—out of the garage and was on his way to the Yard. Although it carried two-way police radio equipment, the Rover was Gideon's private car, not an official Scotland Yard vehicle. Gideon was always glad of that. Had it been official, he would have felt obliged to keep the police radio on all the time. As it was, he felt free to flick on his own private set and listen to

15

the BBC, if he so desired; that was how he had heard that snatch of Penny's concert the night before. This morning, though, he drove in silence, accompanied by nothing but his own thoughts, which became very grim company indeed as he reached the northern end of Fulham, and came within sight of the Wellesley Estate.

Some impulse compelled him to turn the Rover into the Estate, and the next moment he was driving past the trim rows of new houses, all gleaming with fresh paint and all blandly belying the very thought of lawlessness and terror. Until one looked closer and noticed how many of the doors and windows had specially fitted locks and fastenings and how oddly unkempt the front gardens were. (Gardening took courage when at any moment a gang of muggers or hoodlums might come down the street and attack you for daring to be caught outside your own front door.) The farther Gideon drove, the plainer the signs of violence became. He glanced down the once-elegant shopping mall. The windows of half the shops were now boarded up and not one of the mall's lampposts had any bulbs left in them. A white-coated shop assistant was sweeping up glass. Gideon frowned. There shouldn't have been trouble at this particular spot. It was only a hundred yards from a small police substation, and he and Riddell had agreed that this area, the very heart of the Estate, should be kept under police observation at all times. How had the vandals managed to slip past the patrol? Hadn't there been any arrests? The moment he arrived at the Yard, he would get Tom in and demand a report.

By the time Gideon had reached this decision he was passing the Wellesley Community Center, and the three schools: a complex of buildings that had been the planners' crowning pride and achievement. There wasn't much to be proud about now. The schools had boarded-up windows everywhere. In the infants' school playground, swings, seesaw, and roundabouts were all useless wrecks. The gymnasium of the high school—an annex to the main building—was a blackened, burned-out shell. The entrance to the community center was also blackened, as if gas bombs had been lobbed through it. There were signs that the fire brigade had only just stopped the building itself from going up in flames. All of which was reason enough for the center being largely deserted by the community. The foyer was flanked by posters announcing bingo and disco events, but there were "Canceled" notices plastered across them all. The churches seemed to be continuing their services, Sunday morning being perhaps the only relatively safe time during the week.

Gideon was on the point of calling in at the police substation to get an on-the-spot report, but he decided against it. Just because the Wellesley Estate happened to be on his doorstep he had no business poking his nose in and overriding Riddell.

His place was at the Yard, and he had a sudden overwhelming urge to be there. There was plenty of room to turn the Rover in the space outside the community center. It was just as he was slowing down, swinging the wheel to begin the turning operation, that Gideon saw an official-looking notice fastened to a stretch of hardboard covering one of the center's two glassless swing doors.

The notice was typewritten. Gideon had to stop, clamber out, and stride across the pavement before he could make out the wording.

URGENT

Considering the manifest incapacity of the Metropolitan Police Force to restore order to the Wellesley Estate, all residents are invited to attend an EMERGENCY MEETING in the Community Center tonight (Tues. Sept. 10) at 8:30 P.M. for the purpose of setting up a CITIZENS' VIGILANTE FORCE. Don't be afraid to come. In unity is our only safety.

There was no signature, no attempt to identify the organizers of the meeting. Doubtless this could be discovered fast enough as some name must have been given when the hall was booked.

Gideon walked back to his car with a slow, deliberate tread, and as slowly and deliberately drove away. He felt like a man who has been given a savage slap on the face, but who hesitates to retaliate because he has a suspicion that the blow may be deserved.

If he were a resident of the Wellesley Estate, Gideon told himself grimly, by this time *he* would have a thoroughgoing contempt for the law.

2

The Rising Tide

ON COUNTLESS UNCOMFORTABLE occasions in the past, George Gideon's arrival at Scotland Yard had caused storm warnings to be signaled around the departments as soon as he came in sight; but rarely, perhaps never, had his expression betokened trouble so clearly as it did today.

He had no smile whatsoever for the constable who saluted him in the car park and barely replied to the "Good morning, sir" of the sergeant in reception. He made straight for his office, head jutting forward, his massive frame looking as though it was able and ready to bulldoze anyone or anything out of its way. And he had only a grunt to spare for a lean, lanky individual whom he passed on one of the corridors, even though his was a very familiar face indeed. It was Superintendent Lemaitre of N.E. Division, one of the toughest manors in London.

Long years before, Lemaitre had been Gideon's chief assistant. Long years before that, they had been detective sergeants together, and Lemaitre never seemed to forget that they had started their careers on an equal footing. He pointedly refused to treat Gideon with the deference owed to the CID's commander, and Gideon usually let him get away with it, partly for old times' sake, mostly because he was secretly rather sorry for Lem, whose impulsive way of jumping to conclusions had prevented him from getting the full promotion that his agile brain deserved.

Lemaitre clearly had no intention of being dismissed with a grunt.

"Good morning, Gee-Gee. Don't forget I've an appointment with you at ten-thirty, about the Orsini killings. I came up early because I wanted to do some checking with records before I saw you. I'm up against a very peculiar problem over this Orsini business and would like—"

Gideon stopped, turned, and glared.

"When did you say our talk was timed for?"

"Ten-thirty."

Gideon's voice rose in volume.

"Then what the bloody hell do you mean by starting it *now*?"

Lemaitre looked shaken but by no means vanquished. He raised a laconic eyebrow.

"Keep—" he began, and was plainly intending to finish "—your hair on." But at a second glance at Gideon's expression, his temerity deserted him.

His agile wits did not.

"Keep—er-yes, it'll keep, Gee-Gee," he ended hastily. "See you around ten-thirty, then. I'll be—er—looking forward to it."

He disappeared down the corridor with a speed unusually displayed by a senior officer within six years of his retirement age.

Gideon, watching him go, smiled in spite of himself. Good old Lem, he thought, may he never change, and walked on toward his office feeling just a little less like one struck by the wrath of Jehovah.

He had been intending to start the day by summoning Tom Riddell and tearing into him. Now he decided, for both their sakes, to have a quarter-of-an-hour's cooling-off period first. If the Wellesley Estate case was really getting on top of Riddell, if it was pushing him to the brink of cracking up, then a heated exchange would do nothing to help.

But with the unknown vandals seeming to have the complete run of the place, while the police were being openly accused of incompetence on public hoardings, Gideon didn't know how far it was in him to keep the temperature of that interview down.

He went into his office, resisting a childish, but strong, temptation to slam the door behind him. With marked control, he crossed to his polished mahogany desk, seated himself behind it, and began going through the files of new cases and investigations in hand. There weren't many of them.

20

These days, Alec Hobbs sent in only the cases that he considered it vital for his chief to see. The others he dealt with himself, working long and late and hard—so hard that sometimes he and Gideon barely had a chance to exchange more than a few words in the course of a whole working day. Gideon was very grateful to Alec, and never on any occasion had he found his judgment to be wrong; but sometimes he had a guilty feeling that he was being mollycoddled into a sense of false security. If the files on every major case being handled by the CID were put on his desk—as they had been once, when he had first become commander—he knew well enough that the pile would have reached formidable heights every day of the week. The Yard had its successes, sometimes spectacular ones, but by and large, the tide of London crime was rising to a frightening degree.

More frightening in Gideon's eyes was the fall in the age of the average criminal. Children in the ten-to-sixteen age group—ruddy little nippers, as he'd have called them in his own youth—were responsible for 35 percent of all violent snatch-thefts, and 49 percent of burglaries. And that wasn't all they were responsible for. Motiveless maimings, knifings for kicks, the systematic terrorizing of whole neighborhoods could also be put to their discredit. There were some teenagers who were capable of anything, and there seemed to be more of them every day. If things went on at this rate, half of London would end up by being one huge Wellesley Estate.

Gideon forced the thought out of his mind and pounced almost ferociously on the first of the files. It contained the facts on the Orsini killings—the case that Lem was coming to see him about. The Orsinis were two brothers, both of whom had been killed in what appeared to be gangster slayings. The second brother had died after he had proclaimed loudly and publicly that he would avenge his brother's death. Gideon was sure that Lemaitre would announce that he had identified the killer—and then wouldn't have a shred of evidence to back up his suspicions. Jumping to conclusions had always been Lemaitre's main trouble. He had a bad reputation for making premature arrests and must be stopped at all costs from doing it again.

The next file concerned the Cargill case: the kidnapping, six weeks before, of Barbara, the pretty young wife of Gordon Cargill, son of a leading manufacturer, Thomas Cargill of Cargill & Wright's Biscuits. The kidnappers had demanded £50,000 ransom money from Gordon Cargill for the safe return of his wife. With the help of his father, Cargill had found the money, and following the kidnappers' instructions, had left it in the trunk of a secondhand car parked in a side street off the Commercial Road. The police had kept a very, very discreet watch on the pickup point. In fact, they hadn't been physically present in the road at all, but had used sophisticated bugging devices and a TV camera concealed behind the boarded-up window of a derelict newsagent's. But despite all this careful preparation, the kidnappers had been frightened off. The money had not been collected, and nothing further had been heard from the gang. Nothing for six long weeks. Hundreds of possible leads had been followed, involving more police than could easily be spared; but there was no use blinking at the fact that the trail had become cold.

It was getting difficult not to fear the worst for Barbara, and Gideon felt deep sympathy for Matt Honiwell, the chief detective superintendent, who had the triple task of handling the investigation, fighting off an increasingly hostile press, and dealing with the growing despair of the distraught husband and father-in-law. Not that there was anyone at the Yard more suited to the job. Matt's mild appearance concealed not only a penetrating mind but also great depths of human understanding. He would need all that understanding to cope with the atmosphere of spoken and unspoken recrimination—those terrible, inescapable "if onlys"—that always followed when a kidnapping case went wrong.

Gideon turned to a short note that lay beside the files, neatly typed and signed by Alec Hobbs. It confirmed that Lemaitre's appointment was at ten-thirty: Matt Honiwell was down to see him at eleven.

Putting the note on one side, he saw that there was a third file, half-hidden under the others. He pulled it out, and blinked. Never in all his career had he seen a file like this one before. It was a bright pink in color (the ordinary CID files were usually buff) and was inscribed, in Alec's handwriting:

PRIVATE AND PERSONAL.
THE CASE OF THE
BEETHOVEN 2ND.

Abruptly, Gideon remembered that Beethoven's Second Piano Con-

22

certo was the piece that Penny had been playing the night before. Smiling broadly, he opened the file and found a collection of neatly-scissored press cuttings from *The Times,* the *Daily Telegraph,* the *Guardian,* the *Daily Express,* the *Daily Mail*—virtually all that morning's papers. And they made the best reading that he had had in years. "Concert Star Is Born," the *Mail* announced, while the *Times* and the *Telegraph* were full of such resonant drumroll phrases as "flawless technique" and "incomparable phrasing."

Gideon pushed a button. Deputy Commander Alec Hobbs came in, looking, as always, well tailored and distinguished. They spent a happy two minutes reading out the reviews to each other. It would be hard to say which of the two men was the more proud, father or fiancé.

"I'd like to ring Penny and congratulate her now, George," Alec said. "Do you think she'll have got up yet?"

"Oh, she'll be up," Gideon said. "But I should wait a bit, if I were you. She's trying on her wedding dress this morning—I understand a dressmaker's coming to make some alterations. It might be awkward—if not downright bad luck—if you rang her up in the middle of that."

IN POINT OF fact, at that moment Penny Gideon was not trying on her wedding dress, because Marjorie Beresford simply hadn't kept that dress-making appointment.

After waiting a long time, a very slow hour and a half by her bedroom clock, a somewhat indignant Kate telephoned Marjorie to ask why.

For a long time, there was nothing but the ringing tone.

Then there was a click, and she heard Marjorie say, "I—I am sorry. Whoever you are, I can't talk to you now. And I'm afraid all my calls for the day are canceled. I'm—I'm not well."

Kate frowned. There was something startling, even weird, about Marjorie's voice and manner. It was hard to think of any illness that could account for it.

"Look," she said. "This is Kate Gideon. Do you need help of any sort? Should I ring for a doctor?"

"No—no, thank you. I'll manage."

Kate suddenly remembered Marjorie's thirteen-year-old son.

23

"But won't you need some help to cope with Eric when he comes back from school this afternoon?"

Marjorie's voice rose almost to a scream.

"He'll manage. We'll both manage. Leave me alone—*just leave me alone!*"

She rang off, leaving a very puzzled Kate to hang up the receiver.

"What's going on?" called Penny, from the direction of the dining room, where she was enjoying a late breakfast.

"Something I can't make out at all," Kate said, thoughtfully. "Marjorie sounded quite all right when I spoke to her yesterday. Yet now it's as though she's on the point of snapping from some great nervous strain. It's just—not normal."

Penny suddenly had as much trouble finishing her breakfast as her father had had two hours before. She said in a small, unnatural voice, "Is *anything* normal—on that Wellesley Estate?"

3

Signs of Strain

IT WAS AT about that time that Chief Detective Superintendent Riddell walked into Gideon's office, and Gideon and Kate, although six miles apart, shared a common experience: that of sensing themselves to be in the presence of overwhelming strain.

Riddell, a brown-eyed, brown-haired man, had once been as authoritative as Gideon; but the years had not been kind to him, and his once domineering personality had lost much of its impetus. He was still capable of being aggressive and abrasive, could still be implacably determined; but nowadays he could also become deeply anxious when things were going wrong, as though somewhere, at some level inside him, his confidence was faltering. There was no doubt that he was deeply anxious now. His eyes looked haunted; his cheeks were almost gray.

The last of Gideon's earlier fury vanished at the sight of him. He even hated himself for having to begin the interview on a reproachful note, but there was no other honest way.

"Tom, on my way in this morning I took a trip around the Wellesley Estate. And I came across two very disturbing things."

Riddell's lips twisted in a defensive line.

"Only two? I'd say you were lucky."

Gideon's face remained grim.

"First. There had obviously been stone-throwing in that central shopping mall. Now we both agreed that that mall should be guarded night and day."

"We did, and it *was,* George," Riddell said sharply. Clearly his spirit was by no means crushed, however deep his worries went. "There were two detective constables on duty all night, hidden in a supermarket doorway. The trouble was, they were caught by an old playground trick. A gang of boys appeared from nowhere and threw stones at them. The men lost their tempers—not surprisingly as one of them got a nasty gash on his cheek—and, well, the upshot was that they gave chase."

"Out of the mall?"

"Out of the mall, I'm afraid, yes. And immediately, a second gang, that had been waiting around the corner, appeared on the scene and did the damage to the windows. The constables acted very stupidly, of course. As it happens, I was over at Wellesley police station telling them so, at half-past six this morning."

"You were over at Wellesley at—" Gideon took a deep breath. "Tom, don't you ever sleep?"

At this unexpected note of personal concern, Riddell's smile lost much of its bitterness.

"I didn't go over there just for that. I had had a report that someone had been going around the Estate at the crack of dawn, putting up notices about a vigilante force. I thought I ought to look into it pretty damn quick."

Gideon nodded.

"Yes, that was the second thing I was going to ask you about." He suddenly tensed and leaned forward across his desk. What was coming next could be the most important news of the day. "Did you find out who's behind the notices?"

"Without the slightest trouble. He was spotted and recognized by my men several times over while he was putting them up."

"You mean, he's known to the police?"

Riddell almost grinned.

"*And* to everyone on the Wellesley Estate. He's Mr. Harold Neame, headmaster of the local high school. He was putting his notices up at that extraordinary hour for a very sensible reason. He wanted people to see

26

them on their way to work, knowing that if he'd put them up the previous night, vandals would have ripped them to shreds before morning."

Gideon remained tense. It would have been enough of a blow to the police if a vigilante force had been suggested by a crank. But proposed by one of the leaders of the community . . .

"It sounds as though you've been and talked to Neame about it."

"I have. His house is just behind the school. I paid him a call at about seven A.M. and found him in his shirtsleeves, making tea to take up to his wife. He invited me in, gave me a cup, and then suggested I stay for breakfast. . . . He's a good chap really. About fifty. The tall, scholarly type. Mild enough until he gets on the subject of the vandals—and what they've done to his school. Then he rattles away like a machine gun. I've never been given such a lecture on police incompetence in my life. The thought never seemed to occur to him that just *some* of the fault might lie inside his school."

"Never mind about all that," Gideon said impatiently. "The big question, from our point of view, is this: Is Neame acting entirely on his own, or has he got backers in this vigilante enterprise?"

"Backers? From the way he talks, he has the entire Estate behind him. He showed me the names of the vigilante committee. It includes the vicar, the Methodist minister, a Catholic father, the Estate's two doctors, the heads of the other two schools—and a host of quiet, unaggressive people who've come to the end of their tether. After the meeting tonight, when he hopes the force will be set up officially, he intends to apply to the commissioner of Scotland Yard for a special license to issue firearms to its members."

"I can just imagine how Sir Reginald will react to that," Gideon grunted. He got up from his desk and walked to the window. He didn't want Riddell to see the anxiety that must show so plainly on his own face. This situation was developing into one of the gravest crises he had ever faced. Never in the history of Scotland Yard had so many leading members of a community displayed such a lack of confidence in the police. The moment the papers got hold of it, there would be a national outcry; and if the local MP approached the Home Secretary, as he surely would, that would mean a gargantuan top-level inquiry. There was a more serious aspect still. If the Wellesley Estate succeeded in launching its own official vigilantes, other

27

groups would be started in similar trouble-spots up and down the country; and however well-organized or well-disciplined such forces might be, hotheads and extremists were bound to be attracted to their ranks. Britain would be marching down the high road to mob rule; in other words, lynch law.

Gideon's fingers crept instinctively into his pocket and encircled the bowl of a briar pipe that he rarely smoked but kept about him: fondling it, for some reason, soothed and calmed him, helping him to think more clearly.

He turned back to Riddell.

"There's not much doubt what we've got to do, is there? It's absolutely imperative that we both turn up to this meeting at eight-thirty tonight, and at all costs—*at all costs*—restore confidence in the police." All signs of anxiety had been swept from his face, which now glowered pugnaciously. "The only way to do that is the time-honored one. We have to make concrete promises and fulfill them fast. I don't like it any more than you do, but we've *got* to commit ourselves publicly to cracking this case and restoring order within a very short time-limit. Not much more than, say, a week."

Riddell was on his feet now; the desperation in his eyes nakedly apparent.

"George, listen to me! I've been battling with this business *for three months,* and basically, let's face it, got nowhere. What sort of difference will one week make? I have no more idea now than when I started about what the bloody hell I'm up against. I've questioned the few vandals we've arrested—and their parents—for hour after hour after hour, and got nothing definite out of any of them. I've talked to school staffs, doctors, psychiatrists, sociology chaps, and all they've given me is an endless stream of negatives. There is no special racial tension here on the Wellesley Estate, no special color problem, not even an exceptional unemployment rate. There are no extremist groups, right or left, that are particularly active, at least as far as is known. I'm apparently battling with a vast nebulous *nothing*—and yet all my experience suggests that the enemy is, in actual fact, a complex, subtle, highly intelligent *something.* All the violence, even the most piffling little window-smashing incidents, have the hallmark of careful organization and planning. A load of malcontents just creating havoc for kicks simply couldn't have evaded all our precautions so constantly and for so long. And whoever's doing all this organizing and planning has somehow acquired a grip of iron on the minds of just about everyone on the Estate between the ages of, say, thirteen and eighteen . . . *and* the bulk of their parents, too. Sometimes—sometimes I feel I'm in the middle of a science fiction story in which a power from outer space has taken over the bodies and souls of—"

Riddell shrugged and broke off, suddenly realizing the betrayal of his inner state: a state not all that far from hysteria. He managed to smile.

"Sorry, George. I'll be getting the shakes in a minute if I don't watch out."

You never spoke a truer word, Gideon thought grimly. Aloud he said gently, "Tom. Nobody knows better than I do how much you've put into this case. And whenever a copper gives everything he's got to an inquiry for months on end, one of two things happens. Either he gets a nervous breakdown, or he takes a few hours off. *Really* off. Mind wiped clean. So, I want you to regard what I'm saying next as an order. Get to hell out of here for the rest of today. Go home. Go fishing. Do some gardening. Take your wife to the pictures.

"Then, tonight, I want you at my home at seven sharp to be Kate's and my guest for dinner. You and I are going to have a rough time at this meeting. We might as well start the evening in as civilized a way as possible. Don't you agree?"

The expression on the other's face told Gideon that his blend of confidence and sympathy had hit the mark.

His voice unsteady with emotion and relief, Riddell stammered: "This is very good of you, George. But surely I ought to . . ."

Gideon's voice became a roar.

"You ought to be out of here, doing nothing for at least the next ten hours. And don't think or talk a word about Wellesley in all that time. Got it?"

Riddell nodded.

"Then get out. I don't want to see you again until we're both enjoying one of Kate's spectacular dinners."

Grinning gratefully, Riddell moved to the door but turned before he reached it.

"Just one thing, George. That meeting. It's just possible that the vandals—"

"Will use it to stage an attack? Yes, I agree. It's very possible." Gideon found himself thinking aloud, furiously. "But on the other hand, if we pack the hall with uniformed men, we're liable to make the police look a laughingstock—because, basically, it *is* an antipolice meeting. I think the answer is—six uniformed men stationed by the doors, just to remind the people of our presence, and ten to fifteen detectives scattered around the audience. At least two of the detectives should have firearms. Do you agree?"

"Entirely," Riddell said. "I'll see to it before I go." He hesitated for one more second, evidently wondering how to express his thanks again; but Gideon's glare was off-putting. He smiled, turned, and went.

Sighing with relief that he had at least saved one crackpot, Gideon thought grimly of all there was to do. He would have go get someone senior to take over on the Estate case for the day. It was too hot a potato to be left, even temporarily, in junior hands. In addition, he would have to see Sir Reginald Scott-Marle, the commissioner, as soon as possible. In addition, there must be a report, verbal or typewritten, ready for Scott-Marle. In addition, he ought to begin planning the approach he'd take at tonight's meeting. In addition . . .

He glanced at his watch and grimaced.

In addition, it was ten-fifty, which meant that he'd kept Lem waiting for twenty minutes, and now had only ten minutes to deal with the Orsini case before Matt Honiwell came in to discuss the Cargill kidnapping.

Fortunately, long experience had taught Gideon how to divide the day into watertight compartments. The moment Lemaitre came in, all thoughts of Riddell and the Wellesley Estate instantly vanished from his mind, leaving it wholly occupied with the problem of the two Orsini brothers, one of whom had been shot dead within a week of the other, the second after loudly proclaiming that he would avenge the first.

Lem wouldn't have been Lem if he hadn't found some way of stressing how long he'd been cooling his heels in the corridor.

"*What* time did you say our little talk was to begin, Gee-Gee?" he inquired innocently, as soon as he'd been waved to a chair.

"I know, and what the hell do I mean by keeping you waiting," Gideon returned wryly. "Fair point, Lem. Something came up that I couldn't shorten. And I'm afraid I've got to ask you to keep even *this* interview as pithy as you possibly can. It's turning into that sort of day."

Lemaitre, his moment of privileged badinage over, came immediately to the point.

"The layout in a nutshell is this, Gee-Gee. It's increasingly obvious that the Orsinis had those bullets coming to them. They were mixed up in a Mafia-type protection racket, putting the squeeze mostly on restaurants and strip clubs in Soho, but also operating in my manor, all through the Islington–Hornsey area. The head of the racket was, and is, Jack Rocco, who runs a gambling club over in Tottenham and has mysterious connections with clubs all over Soho. The story goes that the first of the Orsinis to die, Nicholas, was rubbed out by, or by order of, Jack Rocco, for the old, old reason—he was keeping too much of his takings. The other Orsini, Mario, was killed because he was blabbing too much, swearing that he'd get Rocco, and so on."

"Are you telling me that you haven't a shred of evidence to support any of this?" Gideon asked quickly.

"Not a shred," Lemaitre admitted cheerfully; then his wiry body tensed. "But yesterday, a man walked into my office with an offer to nail Jack Rocco once and for all . . . *by using himself as a bait.* His name is—Dino Orsini."

Gideon stared.

"Brother of the other two?"

"That's exactly it, Gee-Gee. But Dino's what you'd call the white sheep of the family. He's the kid brother whom the other two Orsinis cosseted. They never let him dabble in anything criminal, but it was with their money that he bought his little business, a successful restaurant over in Finchley, and he reckons he owes them something. So he's offering to do exactly what his brother Mario did. To go to the same bars that Mario went to, swearing that he'll get Rocco in exactly the way Mario did. The difference is, he wants us to cover him and be there when Rocco's hatchet men move in."

Gideon whistled.

"He'll be taking a hell of a risk. Is he a family man?"

"Very much so. Wife and five bambinos. The wife, I gather, practically

31

on her knees begging him to forget the whole thing. I don't mind telling you, Gee-Gee, that I ended up liking this Dino very much. He's one of those fat, black-haired, Italian restaurateurs who are ten a penny round Soho and certainly no hero—or the popular conception of one. By the time he'd got through talking to me, he was quivering like a jelly. But nothing can alter his determination to go through with this. That's what I meant when I told you in the corridor that I was facing a pretty peculiar problem.

"It's not difficult to supply Dino with two night and day bodyguards, but if they stay too close, Rocco will scent a trap and merely bide his time. On the other hand, if they keep their distance, how can they possibly give Dino any kind of real protection? What makes it worse, the man isn't prepared to give us any time. He's determined to start his loudmouthed bar threats tomorrow, while he still has the nerve to do it. It's a frightening situation— like trying to come between a kamikazi pilot and the ground. I've been up in records trying to see if there was some case in the past where the Yard gave a hundred percent protection—completely undetected by the enemy. But so far, I've drawn a blank."

Gideon grinned.

"You weren't looking in the right records, Lem, that's why. Special Branch are the most likely people to have the answer to this one."

"And you're the most likely man to be able to pry it out of them," Lemaitre said. "Will you try, Gee-Gee?"

"I'll try," Gideon promised, "and let's hope it works."

WITH THE APPEARANCE of Matt Honiwell, the atmosphere of strain returned to Gideon's room. Matt was looking in better shape than Riddell, perhaps because he was a considerably younger man. But all the signs of anxiety were there: in his white cheeks, his tired step, his troubled eyes.

He came to the point even faster than Lemaitre had done.

"George, there's been an odd development in this Cargill business, and I may have made a rather silly decision. Over these last weeks, I've become very friendly with both Gordon Cargill and his father. We're on pretty confidential terms."

Gideon nodded. This, he told himself, was the most striking evidence of the power of Matt's humanity. Other families in the Cargills' position would have been deeply suspicious of the police, and perhaps downright hostile, by now. But Matt had won them over—and Gideon knew how. Matt would have sweated and suffered alongside them all the way.

"This morning," Matt went on quietly, "Gordon confided to me, as a friend rather than a Yard man, that they were thinking of approaching a seer."

Gideon started violently. That was the last word he was expecting. He wondered, in fact, if he had heard right.

"A—seer?"

"Yes. You know. An extrasensory perception man, a clairvoyant, a—"

"Thanks," Gideon said tartly. "I have an English dictionary somewhere in the desk, as it happens. I do occasionally read it."

Matt ran a hand through his still plentiful brown hair, suppressing a smile as he went on blandly, "The man they are consulting is a Czech called Jacob Brodnik, a naturalized Briton who lives in Maxwell Grove, West Dulwich. He often works on the Continent, I believe. The Belgian police, the Dutch, and the French Sûretè have all used him at one time or another as, I think it's called, a corpse-diviner."

"You frighten me," Gideon said drily. "Does Barbara Cargill *have* to be written off as a corpse?"

"I've told both Gordon and his father that after six weeks of hearing nothing from the kidnappers, it's a possibility that has to be faced," said Matt, his voice deliberately matter-of-fact. "They're prepared to accept the worst, if worst it is. What they find unbearable is the tension, the not knowing. They're hoping that this Brodnik, if nothing else, can sense if she's alive or dead."

"H'm," Gideon said. "When are they going to see him?"

"Gordon's off to Dulwich tonight. He has an appointment with Brodnik at eight. He asked me if I'd go with him—to hold his hand, as he put it. Without thinking, I said that I would. It was only later that I realized that I might have made a major blunder. If the papers get hold of this, they might take the line that Scotland Yard was officially calling in a seer. Every tabloid paper in Britain would go to town on it."

"They couldn't—if you make it clear that you're only going as an impartial observer," Gideon said judiciously. "No, Matt. Your real difficulties will come later. Supposing this Brodnik 'sees' Barbara's body lying in a certain wood or hidden in a certain house? The Cargills will expect us to

33

investigate, but *we won't be able to.* No matter what the Belgians or the Dutch may do, I simply can't allow the valuable time of valuable men to be expended on ESP wild-goose chases."

Matt's face hardened.

"Do you really think I'd ask you to?" he said drily.

Gideon took a deep breath. It seemed to be a morning for dealing with men at the end of their tether.

"All I'm pointing out," he said quietly, "is that if you go to this Brodnik session, you might be under very great emotional pressure to make such a request. And I'm warning you in advance that my answer would have to be 'no.' With that reservation, you can go to this meeting with my blessing." His voice softened. "And incidentally, you can tell Gordon Cargill something from me."

"And what is that?"

Gideon, for once, pulled his briar pipe out of his pocket. He stood, staring down at it, turning it over in his hands.

"As a man, not as a policeman, I sympathize with what he's doing. If Kate had been kidnapped, and I hadn't heard anything for six weeks, I'm not sure I wouldn't be queuing up to see this Brodnik myself."

GIDEON STAYED LIKE that, staring down at his pipe, for a full minute after Matt Honiwell had gone. It was hard to remember a morning when he had had quite so many strange and harrowing problems to solve.

How to afford a man invisible, yet a hundred percent effective, protection against a gangster's bullets.

How to cope with the incalculable results of a seer's vision on a kidnapping case.

How to halt a vigilante movement in its tracks . . . and convince the residents of an Estate that had been torn apart by violence for three months that he could restore law and order in a week.

It was the last problem that demanded priority.

Gideon seated himself heavily behind his desk and began to make notes—partly for a report to Scott-Marle, partly for a plan of action to be carried out that night.

He wished devoutly that he had some of the alleged powers of Jacob

Brodnik. He would have given a year's salary for a moment's insight into what was really at the back of the violence on the Wellesley Estate.

ONE THING THAT was really happening there was that Marjorie Beresford was lying on the bed in her son's room, shaking with silent sobs.

She had been lying there for hours now and had only gone downstairs once—to answer Kate Gideon's telephone call and to ring her various customers, canceling appointments for the day.

When she returned, she had drawn the curtains, so that she could lie in the dark with her grief, her deeply felt sense of shame.

Marjorie was not only the widow of a policeman; she was the daughter of one. Law and order had been part of her life from the day she was born.

So nothing had prepared her for the shock she had received at about eight o'clock that morning.

Eric, her son, had left home unusually early, at around seven forty-five. He had said he wanted to see a friend about something before he went on to school.

Marjorie had decided to tidy his room straight away, before she went out to keep her eight-thirty appointment at the Gideons'.

It was while she was making Eric's bed that she had suddenly felt one of the floorboards creak beneath her feet.

Thinking it needed a nail, she had gone down on her knees to examine it and found that it came right up in her hands.

Peering into the cavity, she had seen a number of objects carefully concealed within it, objects that, with all her experience of the police, she recognized on sight.

A stocking, stretched and shapeless, as if after use as a face mask.

A cosh.

A flick knife.

A white shirt stained with blood.

It was the shirt that swam before her eyes now, in the artificial gloom of that curtained room. It was Eric's shirt, there was no doubt of that.

But Eric had not cut himself, or sustained any serious injury that she knew of, in his life.

So whose, whose, *whose* was all that blood?

And what, what, *what,* in God's name, should she do about it?

35

Ring the police and tell them that her thirteen-year-old son was a mugger, perhaps a murderer? Unthinkable. Destroy the evidence that would make herself an accessory after the fact? For a policeman's widow, equally out of the question.

This much was sure. She must confront Eric with what she had found; try to talk it over; try to understand . . .

If only he hadn't been so withdrawn lately.

If only the world hadn't suddenly become such a strange, incomprehensible place.

If only, for example, this room would stop swirling around . . .

If only there wasn't this mist in front of her eyes, the color of that bloodstained . . .

She must get help, somehow, somewhere.

She staggered off the bed, to the landing, then, clinging to the banisters, reached the hall where the telephone was.

Without quite realizing what she was doing—out, in fact, of a deep subconscious compulsion—she started to dial a number.

But she stopped herself after the first three digits.

What on earth had she been thinking of—trying to ring the *Gideons'* home?

4

Crimson Light

BY HALF-PAST SEVEN, the sinking September sun, touched by an early autumn mist, was spreading over London an air of unreality, changing the Thames into a mystical river of fire. Even the placid, redbrick houses of Harringdon Street, Fulham, had been affected, turned to a vicious crimson.

It was, in fact, a nightmare sunset; a sunset to heighten tension, deepen fear.

Yet inside No. 20 Harringdon Street, the mood was cheerful and relaxed. Despite her hectic day of wedding preparation, Kate had found time to rustle up the most sumptous of lobster salads to set before Gideon and Tom Riddell, and a bottle of Sauterne to wash it down. Gideon was surprised and relieved to see that Tom tackled the food with relish; his ten hours off the case had evidently done him good. Gideon himself was suddenly equally ravenous.

Seeing them eating so heartily, no one would have imagined that within an hour they were due to attend a crucial confrontation; but it was that very fact that was putting an edge on their appetites. However formidable the vigilante meeting might be, it at least held a promise of action, which was something of a relief after the long months of baffled, fruitless conjecture. In a curious way, Gideon was looking forward to it.

He hadn't forgotten that he, and the whole Metropolitan Police Force, were going to be under heavy fire; that the consequences, if his arguments failed to win the day, would be dire. But Gideon had no intention of losing the day. He even had a surprise proposition to spring, if the worst came to the worst; and for this he had obtained Scott-Marle's permission.

In short, he was ready for the fray and, as positive proof of the fact, was more than ready to tuck into Kate's lobster salad.

NOT EVERYONE WAS facing the future with such confidence in the forbidding light of that September sunset.

While Gideon and Riddell were happily eating, six miles away across London, Dino Orsini was carrying two plates full of lasagne verde to a young couple at the corner table of his flashy little restaurant in Finchley.

He stumbled as he walked; the plates nearly fell, and his plump, creamy cheeks turned nearly as green as the lasagne.

The young couple watched him curiously. The girl stifled a giggle, while the man told himself righteously that this fat little Italian should go on a diet. Such a lack of briskness surely showed an over-liking for his own spaghetti.

"Excusa me, pliss," Dino murmured. "Ees hot night. And I am clumsee fool."

Dino often talked broken English for his customers. It contributed to the jolly atmosphere he tried to create in his restaurant; an atmosphere of winks, nudges, and chortles by candlelight, in keeping with the motto printed on the menus: *Eat good—and feel good—at Dino's.*

Tonight, though, he was finding it almost impossible to sustain his role. Mental images of his brothers flitted before him, Nicholas and Mario, lying dead from the Rocco gang's bullets; and then came the inevitable wondering what it would feel like when bullets were pumped into his own body.

This was the last evening he would be serving in this restaurant. Tomorrow night, his wife, Vittoria, would take over, while he, Dino, would be in a certain bar in Soho, where his brother Mario had been a regular, and where every whisper went straight to Jack Rocco's ears. He wouldn't be talking broken English there. He'd be pouring out a stream of voluble Italian, every word calculated to challenge and enrage Rocco. After that, he could expect a call from Jack's hatchet men any moment of the night or day; and he was under no illusions about how difficult it would be for Mr. Lemaitre to protect him. Vittoria was right. It was a mad thing he was embarking on, he was all kinds of a fool not to back out.

But beneath Dino's overgenerous layer of quivering flabbiness was a determination of iron. If his death was the only way by which a murder charge could be brought against Rocco, then it was a matter of family duty that he should die. It was as simple as that. He must not allow the thought of Vittoria and the children to come into it.

He breathed a silent prayer for strength; and as he prayed he instinctively started to cross himself. He forgot that he was still holding a plate of lasagne in each hand. This time, one of them actually slipped and fell to the floor, missing the girl he was serving by inches.

"*Sacramento! Mama mia!* I deserve-a to be . . ."

He was about to add "shot," but the word stuck in his throat.

He put the remaining plate on the table with a far from steady hand, and disappeared through the swing doors leading to the kitchen quarters.

Behind him, he heard suppressed laughter on all sides; and when he accidentally cannoned into one of the waiters, and sent more plates crashing, the laughter grew louder still.

What was wrong with that, he asked himself. People were supposed to "eat good and feel good" at Dino's. And a moment later, the roars of laughter proved very useful. They drowned the sound of funny fat Dino being violently sick.

A LONG WAY south of Finchley and some miles east of Fulham lies the quiet, leafy suburb of Dulwich. Here a man was facing the future with neither confidence nor terror, but with the gray emptiness of despair.

Gordon Cargill was almost certain that the corpse-diviner Brodnik was going to confirm the fact that his wife, Barbara, was dead. Was there, then, any real need for him to keep this painful appointment? Hadn't he been through agony enough?

He slowed his car, an elegant, black Bentley, down to walking pace as he turned into Maxwell Grove. If Jacob Brodnik's notepaper was to be believed, the famous ESP man lived along here, at No. 4.

The Grove looked about right for a corpse-diviner's home. The whole place had the air of being a crumbling monument to a dead era, when to live in S.E. 21 meant that your household boasted a cook, a nanny, and at least one chambermaid. There were only six houses in the street. Each was detached, standing well back in its own grounds. Each had a wide drive leading up to, and away from, its front door. But there the atmosphere of munificence ended. All the front doors in the road badly needed a coat of paint. All the drives were covered with weeds. Of the six houses, four had been converted into flats or maisonettes, one had an empty, waiting-for-demolition look, and one—half its windows boarded up—was positively derelict.

It was this derelict house that was numbered "4."

Plainly, Jacob Brodnik cared so little for the things of this world that he had let his own home fall into ruins—camping in it, presumably, like a squatter. The man was surely mad, and he, Cargill, had been mad to come.

He slowed the Bentley to a halt. His face—a smooth, young, business-executive face, handsome, boyishly determined, but with a far older man's shadows under the eyes—became grim and angry.

"Well, that's it, Matt," he said. "One lunatic is enough. I'm going home."

Chief Detective Superintendent Matt Honiwell, in the seat beside him, grunted.

"Now that you've dragged me all this way, you might as well go through with the thing."

Gordon Cargill leaned back behind the wheel and eyed Honiwell quizzically.

"That's a surprising line for you to take. I'd rather gathered that this whole enterprise of mine was an acute embarrassment to Scotland Yard."

Honiwell put on his friendliest grin.

"Scotland Yard doesn't lose face all that easily, nor do I. I might tell you that quite a few Yard men, from Commander Gideon down, have a sneaking sympathy for you for calling Brodnik in. When every human effort fails, it takes a rather unusual man to try—superhuman ones."

Gordon smiled bitterly.

"Nice to know that. But sympathy falls a little short of *support*, doesn't it? You've made it crystal clear that even if Brodnik did give us a lead, the Yard couldn't spare the time or the men to follow it up. So is there really any point in going on?"

Honiwell hesitated. For a moment, he was tempted to advise Gordon to turn back; it would save the Yard a lot of trouble if he did. But Matt didn't like the note of bitterness in Gordon's voice. It was the first hint of anger against the police that he had so far shown, through all this agonizing inquiry. Nor did he like the total helplessness in his eyes. It was, Matt decided, healthier for a drowning man to clutch at a straw than to let himself, despairingly, sink. He, at all events, wasn't going to be the one to snatch it away.

"Listen, sir," he found himself saying. "If you turn back now, you're going to spend the rest of your life with the thought that you didn't do *everything* possible to find your wife. And if I encourage you to go back, then—don't you see?—*I'm* going to have to live with it, too."

Matt was surprised, even alarmed, at his own vehemence. Gideon had warned him to accompany Gordon Cargill on this mission as an impartial observer only. Just how impartial could anyone call *this?*

His words, at all events, had done the trick. The hopelessness had gone from Gordon's eyes, the bitterness from his smile.

"You're really quite a copper, aren't you, Matt?" he said, his tone instantly restoring the odd friendship that had grown up between them over the past harrowing weeks. "Whether you're a good one or not, only God and Scotland Yard know. But I'll take your advice, and on your own head be it. Brodnik, here we come!"

He started up the Bentley and swung it into the weed strewn drive of No. 4.

IT WAS ON the Wellesley Estate that the reddened sun had the most impact. All the bright white concrete was turned a garish crimson, creating a surrealist landscape, a visual shriek of terror. Everybody sensed instinctively that trouble was ahead tonight; but in a hundred different houses men and women were deciding at last that the time had come to act against it. In a moment, they'd be heading for the vigilante meeting, resolved to join in a great roar of outrage against the police and to make a unanimous demand for an alternative method of enforcing the law.

In many other houses, there was no such determination—only a conspiracy of silence and fear.

And in one house there was stark hysteria. The hysteria of a woman who had lost the power to face the future on any terms at all.

41

Marjorie Beresford had spent the morning and afternoon wondering what she would say to her son when he came home from school.

It had never occurred to her that he might not come home at all.

He should have been back by four. When five o'clock came, then six, then seven, she was reduced to walking around and around the house in an agony of bewildered despair. Ordinarily she would have rung up the school long since and then telephoned the parents of Eric's friends for news. Perhaps by now she'd have called the police. But guilt, and the knowledge of what Eric might—must—have done, had somehow induced a kind of paralysis in her. Supposing Eric had been found out and was on the run?

No, that wasn't possible; the police would have called.

Perhaps, then, he'd joined up with a gang—was about to become involved in more of this crazy, stupid, bloody violence . . .

Bloody. She thought of the shirt, the knife . . .

Her brain whirling, Marjorie went to the front door and, for the twentieth time in as many minutes, peered down the road in the desperate hope that she might see Eric coming.

The sun shone in her eyes. The red, red sun that seemed to be turning everything to blood.

Something snapped in her mind.

She couldn't stand this any more, she had to talk to someone, get advice.

The telephone was just behind her in the hall. Exactly as she had done that morning, she found herself dialing the Gideons' home. Only this time she didn't stop at the first three digits. She finished dialing and got right through.

Since Gideon and Riddell had just left for the meeting, it was Kate who listened calmly, quietly, while Marjorie poured out—in an unstoppable, only just audible, torrent of words—the first inside report that had come from the Estate of fear.

5

The Walkers

GIDEON'S MOOD OF brisk confidence did not long survive, once his Rover turned into the Wellesley Estate. The crimson sunset was fading now, but in its place had come a strange twilight overhung by an eerie redness, as though some great fire was blazing somewhere just out of sight. The tension in the air was almost tangible, and Gideon didn't have to look far to see the cause. The pavements on both sides of the road were thronged with people streaming in the direction of the community center. And there was something odd about these people. Few were strolling along, idly chatting, as one might expect, seeing that the center was only a minute's walk away, and there was half an hour to go before the meeting. Most were walking quickly, purposefully, *angrily* through the weird red dusk.

Some were even carrying weapons, or objects that could be used as such. Gideon saw three youngish men with walking sticks, perhaps borrowed from old uncles or grandfathers. Others had heavy car torches. Of course, thought Gideon, to be out and about on the Wellesley Estate after dark took considerable courage.

Watching these angry walkers, Gideon began not only to understand their mood but to share it, and to know how close it came to fury.

"Tom," he said drily, "this is going to be one hell of a meeting. If this Harold Neame is any sort of an orator he can convert this lot into a full-scale lynch mob with a flick of his finger."

Riddell pulled out a handkerchief and wiped his face. The night was hot and humid.

"I don't think Neame's quite that type," he said. "Oh, he's sincere enough and angry enough. But he's been a headmaster too long for effective rabble-rousing. He barked at me this morning as though he expected me to take a hundred lines. If he talks to the audience that way, I don't think it will be difficult to win them over to our side."

Gideon shook his head. "I'm not so sure. When people get scared and desperate, it's very easy to turn that fright and desperation into hate, and easiest of all to turn it into hatred of the police. That's the game Neame's been playing, and even though he disguises it under a plea for law and order, it's the most lawless game in the world. Don't you realize? These people all around us: they're the respectable folk, the people we'd ordinarily rely on, the people who make policing possible, and who have always turned to us for help. And tonight they're going to that hall to attack us, jeer at us, shout us down! And if trouble starts—and from the look of those faces, I've no doubt that some sort of trouble will—who can tell whose side the majority will be on?"

"I can," Riddell said confidently. "They'll be on yours. You're forgetting something. That there's no crowd of citizens, respectable or otherwise, that can shout George Gideon down."

Gideon didn't smile.

"Thank you for those few kind words," he said wearily. "Forgive me if I forget 'em—fast. I was a sight too smug earlier this evening—and smugness is our deadliest enemy tonight. If I'm to win these people over, I've got to put every bloody thing I have into what I say—and I wish I could overcome the feeling that, even so, it may not be enough. If only—"

He broke off, startled to find Riddell picking up his train of thought as precisely as though it were his own.

"If only we had one tangible clue as to what was really happening here," he said. "To tell you the truth, George, I'm not too concerned about the people who are turning out to this meeting. They're the ones with nothing to hide; they're just motivated by a blazing bewilderment about what's been happening all around them. It's the *other* people on the Estate I'm frightened about. The ones who'll be staying at home behind drawn curtains and bolted doors, terrified to move or speak because of—because of *what*?" In the gloom, Riddell's face was suddenly a gleaming mask of sweat. His day off, followed by that relaxed dinner at the Gideons', had undoubtedly done him good; but now that good was being eroded at an alarming rate. He was already almost as jumpy as he had been in Gideon's office at the beginning of the day. What he'd be like by the end of the evening . . .

"Steady," Gideon said quietly, his voice giving no hint of the decision he'd just reached that Riddell simply had to come off this case. "Remember what I said this morning about taking time off. You're due for leave, and I'll see you get it."

Riddell tried to laugh, but the sound was hoarse and strained.

"I also remember what you said about breakdowns. Wouldn't it be just my luck if that came first?"

Gideon, having no answer, concentrated with unnecessary caution on his driving.

They had arrived in High Street, passing through the battered shopping mall, the shop windows dark behind protective boarding. The small police substation was some yards ahead, and beyond that loomed the community center and the three schools. Clearly, not all Wellesley's citizens were walking to the meeting. Although it was still only just past eight, the center's small car park was jammed full, while in front of the center itself were parked BBC and ITV news vans, their cables trailing inside the building. Gideon's heart sank at the sight of them. If this vigilante movement got massive publicity from the outset, it could become a national conflagration within days . . . It was more than ever important for him to stop it at the onset. He remembered the surprise proposition he'd discussed with Scott-Marle, to be used "if the worst came to the worst." There was little doubt in his mind that such a condition would soon become inevitable.

In order to avoid an encounter with TV reporters, most of whom knew him by sight, Gideon decided to stop outside the police station and walk the remaining fifty yards to the center. He could get someone to park the Rover in the police station yard, which he remembered was fairly sizable.

He pulled up, and he and Riddell alighted. At that moment a large black Triumph nosed its way out of the yard. It was an area patrol car, with a uniformed sergeant and constable occupying the front seat, and a loutish looking youth clad in jeans and a denim jacket at the back. The loutish looking youth would be, in reality, a detective constable—a DC—clearly a very young one; a lad who had served some years in uniform on the beat, and now, fresh from Hendon College, was anxious to prove himself in plainclothes work. Area patrol cars operated to a standard routine. If any suspicious activity was spotted, the car itself would drive on by; but the DC would nip out of the farside door and try and get a closer look at what was going on. He would have a walkie-talkie concealed on him, so that he could keep in unobtrusive contact with the car, which would have stopped around the next corner, and be waiting to hear from him.

On a sudden impulse, Gideon strode up to the car. Even in the poor light, the sergeant recognized him instantly. The car stopped. The sergeant saluted and wound down the window.

"Good evening, sir."

"Good evening, sergeant. There's no special trouble on the Estate, is there?"

"No, sir. There are dozens of people on the streets, presumably proceeding to the community center, but so far, the reports say that they're all behaving in an orderly manner."

Lower-rank policemen, talking to Gideon for the first time, often took refuge in witness-box phraseology. Somehow it always made Gideon adopt formal language, too.

"Right," he said. "Make sure you keep a sharp eye on all these walkers, sergeant. I have a strong suspicion that somewhere among them you'll find a disorderly element—teenage toughs under instructions to try and break up the meeting."

"Don't you worry, sir," the sergeant said comfortably. "If we find any such people about, we'll apprehend them immediately."

"No," Gideon said.

"I—beg your pardon, sir?"

"No apprehending, sergeant. Just keep an eye on them, and, if possible, get your observer in among them. I'm out to stop trouble, of course. But *finding out who's causing it* is by far the most important. And by infiltration there's always a chance your man might pick up a scrap of conversation that could tell us a lot."

"I understand, sir," the sergeant said, a trifle gruffly.

46

Gideon turned his attention to the young man in the back of the car. On closer inspection, he looked far from being the lout he represented. His eyes were keen and alert as he flashed Gideon what was almost a mischievous grin. Gideon took an instant liking to him. A cool customer, he told himself, and obviously bright. Ought to go far in the force, unless he became restless at the discipline, as so many of that type did. Incidentally, there was something familiar about this face . . .

"What's your name, son?"

"Detective Constable Rowlandes, sir, 563."

"I'd sooner have your Christian name than your number."

"In that case, sir, it's John."

"H'm. You're not the son of Malcolm Rowlandes, by any chance?"

The young man's grin vanished. In its place was a look of surprise, mixed with a certain degree of awe.

"My father's name is Malcolm, sir, yes."

Gideon smiled.

"One of the best detective inspectors this division ever had. I was always sorry he left the force so young. He's security officer for Omega Insurance now, isn't he?"

Rowlandes looked back with a growing respect. His father had retired all of eight years before. That the great Commander Gideon should not only remember him, but where he was working now . . .

"That's quite correct, sir."

"Give him my regards," Gideon said. "And good luck tonight, Rowlandes. If you do succeed in getting in among the enemy, it could be crucial to this case. But leave that walkie-talkie behind when you get out of the car. If it were spotted, it could be your death warrant. Is that quite clear?"

"Very clear indeed, sir."

"Then off you go."

The sergeant in front saluted again; the area car drove off. Gideon had one last quick glimpse of John Rowlandes's face staring back at him out of a rearside window. The boy was grinning again, not mischievously now, but more like a child who'd been handed a surprise Christmas present by a Santa Claus in the street. No doubt he was preening himself on having been picked for a dangerous special assignment by the commander of the whole CID. Gideon hoped it wouldn't go to his head.

"Excuse me, sir."

Gideon looked around. A sergeant had come hurrying out of the station to speak to him—a fat, fiftyish sergeant, obviously in bad condition: even this tiny spring had made him short of breath.

"Mrs. Gideon," he panted. "On the . . . on the phone, sir. Wants to speak to you . . . very urgently. Suddenly thought . . . she might reach you . . . here . . ."

But Gideon had long since started striding toward the station entrance. Within five seconds, he was inside talking to Kate and hearing the whole of Marjorie Beresford's story.

When he came out, he walked straight up to Riddell and outlined all that he had heard.

Riddell had rarely seen him look so cock-a-hoop.

"I think this is the breakthrough, Tom. The wall of silence you've been facing has had a brick blasted right out of its center. And from now on, the answers to your questions should be coming thick and fast."

Riddell stared.

"Because a poor wretched woman suspects her son of being a mugger?"

"No. Because she's had the courage—or the hysteria, I don't know which you'd call it—to come straight to the police about it. Don't you see? That's just what *far too many other people on the Estate haven't done.*"

"You mean . . ."

"Work it out for yourself, Tom. Here we have an area afflicted by an overwhelming outbreak of highly organized juvenile crime. At the same time we find dozens of families refusing to talk; obstructing the police in every way they can. Put the two things together in the light of what's happened to Marjorie Beresford—and the situation is all too clear.

"We're up against an organization that has found a way of getting children into its clutches at an extraordinarily young and tender age. And it doesn't play games with these children. Perhaps as a matter of deliberate policy, it plunges them into deep trouble—quick. In that way, it reduces parents to a state of moral paralysis. If they come near the police, they're faced with the unbearable prospect of their own boys, who were perfectly normal, good lads until a few weeks ago, being snatched away from them and sent to Borstal Prison for the rest of their teens, if not longer.

"That's what we're fighting, Tom—the perfectly natural desire of loving

48

parents to protect their children from the unthinkable. And behind that, there's a gang—or a movement, or an individual—with a frightening power to get decent kids to behave in such a way that the parents' hands are tied.

"But now we are in a position to act. Or rather—" Gideon corrected himself gruffly, "*I* am. I'm sorry about this, Tom, this is your inquiry, and you should be conducting the investigation. But since Marjorie Beresford came to Kate and me—"

"You feel you're the person who ought to go and see them," Riddell said evenly. "And you're right, of course, George. I'll keep your place at the meeting." His tension began to show again as he added nervously, "Please don't be too late coming to it."

"I won't," Gideon promised. "Oh, and if Neame starts speaking before I'm there, could you take a few notes? I'd like to answer him point by point."

Riddell promised to do this, and Gideon walked back to the Rover. With one finger on the door handle, he stopped and turned.

"Marjorie Beresford's house is in Wellington Road. Would that be far?"

"No, it's just on the left past the shopping mall. Two hundred yards at the most."

"Then I might as well copy the locals, and walk," Gideon grunted. "See you later, Tom."

And he was off along High Street, striding away from the community center as purposefully as everyone else was walking toward it. Not that this gave rise to any difficulties. When Gideon made up his mind to go somewhere, people instinctively stepped out of his way.

GIDEON FOUND MARJORIE Beresford's road without difficulty and turned into it. At exactly that moment, in another road turning off High Street, the police patrol car spotted a group of ten or twelve youths walking in the direction of the community center.

There was no hint of rowdiness in their behavior. Their progress was slow, measured, almost sedate, as if they were under orders to behave quietly and look respectable. Their clothes were above reproach; almost incongruously so. As far as the sergeant could see in the gloom, they were all wearing smart, two-piece suits. They might have been going to a wedding, rather than a meeting.

That settled it, as far as the sergeant was concerned.

When a gang of Wellesley Estate yobs got dressed up like that, there *had* to be something brewing. And that slow, calculated walk of theirs was beginning to look as menacing as a mock funeral march.

"This is it, Rowlandes," the sergeant said. "We'll slow down at the corner and out you go."

In the back of the car, DC John Rowlandes tensed and got ready to open the rear door.

"Sorry you've got to leave your walkie-talkie," the sergeant said. "But we'll stay within earshot as far as we can."

"That's right, lad," the driver said helpfully. "Just give one 'orrible scream, and we'll be along in no time to pull the knife out of your back and mop up your blood from the pavement."

Rowlandes grinned—just a little uneasily.

"That'll be enough of that, Hodgson," the sergeant barked at the driver.

It *had* to be enough; there was no time for anything more to be said at all. The car had swept well past the youths, and was already at the corner of the street. This part of the Estate, like so many other parts, had been left poorly lighted because of vandal-wrecked lamp standards. Rowlandes jumped out into a deep pool of shadow and felt sure that, even if one of the youths had been glancing back, his leap couldn't have been seen.

He straightened up, aware that his heart was beating faster than usual as he hurried along the pavement in the wake of the youths. At the sound of his footsteps behind them, several turned.

"You with us, mate?"

The question told Rowlandes that this wasn't one of those intimate gangs, in which every member was known to the rest by sight. He decided to take a chance.

"Yeah," he said. "Sorry I'm late."

"You're not only late, you've got the wrong gear on. Didn't you get the order? No jeans—no denims. We're going to a pig meeting, aren't we? Gotta dress like pigs and straights."

Suddenly—as though suspicion was blazing up in all their minds simultaneously—the gang stopped walking. So did Rowlandes. It is hard

50

to make progress, even at a funeral march pace, when one's arms are pinioned behind one's back and a flick knife is held to one's face.

"How come you didn't know those orders—if you're one of us?"

Rowlandes found to his surprise that the lump in his throat had vanished. It was as though nature realized that he'd be lost if he showed fear and was giving him the chance to speak clearly. Rowlandes made the most of it. His voice rose in a snarl of aggression.

"I know the orders a bloody sight better than you do, matie. We were told not to arouse suspicion, weren't we? Do you call *this* not arousing suspicion?"

The gang tensed.

"Keep your voice down, you fool," the brandisher of the flick knife said.

Rowlandes lowered his tone only slightly.

"Then put that thing away. Save it for the pig meeting. It's proper use is for carving pork."

That line had been an inspiration. It was greeted by guffaws on all sides. Suspicion, like the flick knife, vanished as though it had never been. Rowlandes's arms were released, and a moment later he found himself turning into High Street almost in the vanguard of the gang.

Halfway along High Street the patrol car came out of a side turning and shot past them. Rowlandes's heart jumped. The nits, he thought; they'd promised to keep in earshot, not in sight. Already he could sense some members of the gang eyeing him thoughtfully, perhaps beginning to put two and two together . . .

Suddenly an idea occurred to him—an idea he considered worthy of a detective on a special mission from Commander Gideon himself.

He waved derisively at the area patrol car and bellowed after it, "Up the vigilantes!"

To the others, he murmured coolly, "Now the bloody fuzz will be *sure* we're bleeding pigs!"

INSIDE THE AREA patrol car, the startled sergeant pushed his cap to the back of his head.

"Either Rowlandes will finish up the night with a police medal," he told his driver, "or your guess will turn out right. We *will* be pulling a knife out of his back and mopping up the blood."

"I SUPPOSE IT couldn't be *animals'* blood, Mr. Gideon?"

Gideon turned Eric Beresford's shirt over in his hands and found it hard to meet Marjorie's pleading eyes.

"It's possible," he said shortly. "But I think we'd both be fooling ourselves if we didn't admit that the odds are heavily against it."

Marjorie Beresford nodded. She was perfectly calm now; rather too calm for Gideon's liking. Her small, plain face—on which the lines of her tragic life showed all too plainly—was chalk-white, except for a doll-like spot of color on each cheek.

"Does this mean you'll be putting Eric under arrest?"

Gideon was a long, long time replying, and during the pause, he had even greater difficulty in meeting Marjorie's eyes.

They were dead now, rather than pleading. Obviously she was asking herself over and over again how she could have done this thing to her own son. And Gideon couldn't help asking himself what action *he* would have taken if one of his own boys at the age of thirteen had been thus embroiled. It was unthinkable, of course, that any of the three—now long since grown-up and launched on successful careers—would ever have taken part in violence of this sort. But then he, Gideon, hadn't been killed when they were only five or six. And they had never been exposed to the mysterious evil that was spreading its tentacles over the Wellesley Estate . . .

All around him, here in Eric's bedroom, was evidence that the boy was basically a normal child. School exercise books were scattered untidily about, as they were in thousands of other schoolboys' bedrooms. One of them, an English book, was lying open. Eric, seemingly, had scored only two out of ten for an essay on "What I Did During the Summer Holidays." There was a note in red ink from an outraged English master: Disgraceful work. See me. G.M.H.

From the cover of the book, Gideon noted that Eric was in Form IIIB of Wellesley High School, a school in which Harold Neame was head . . .

He glanced around at the rest of the room: at the pop posters on the walls; at a pile of model airplane kits; at the row of beautifully made Spitfires and Hurricanes on the mantelpiece. Not just a normal child, he thought, but a talented one, English essays apart. Gideon had always admired people who were good with their hands . . .

From all this normality, he turned back to nightmare: that menacing hole in the floorboards from which the flick knife, the stocking mask, the shirt had come.

"You haven't answered my question," Marjorie said tonelessly. "Will Eric be arrested?"

Gideon decided that bluntness would be, in the end, the kindest course. He was talking to a policeman's widow. She wouldn't be fooled by prevarication.

"I certainly can't promise anything," he said. "All I can tell you is that a great many children on this Estate are as deeply involved in this nightmare as he is. And a great many parents are sharing your agony. The only difference being, that they haven't had the guts to do what you did. Don't ever think it's going to go worse for Eric because you came to me. On the contrary, if he answers our questions fully and honestly, I will do all I can to help him. He could be the instrument for ending this whole evil business. And if he is, that won't be forgotten—whatever he's done."

Marjorie looked slightly, but only very slightly, reassured. The high points of feverish color spread out across her cheeks, lessening her pallor, giving her an almost schoolgirlish flush. Womanlike, she seized on the last line of Gideon's speech and twisted it.

"That means you're sure he's done something terrible."

Gideon took a deep breath.

"How can anyone say what he's done until we've got him here, and talked to him? In the meantime, if *you* wouldn't mind answering a few questions . . ."

He asked her about Eric's friends, habits, daily routine. He discovered what he might have suspected: that Eric had his doting mother firmly under his thumb. He rarely mentioned his friends, hardly ever brought them home to the house. If he wanted to go out in the evening, out he went, and not all Marjorie's pleadings about mobs and muggers had availed at all. He had been out with "the gang," as he called them, between eight and eleven on most nights in the past month and had never vouchsafed any information about where they'd been. Marjorie had been too thankful to see him home again safe and sound to question him closely.

"It never occurred to me that the reason he and his friends were safe was because . . ."

"*They* were the mobsters and muggers?" Gideon suggested gently.

53

Suddenly she was back where she'd been most of the day—on the very edge of hysteria.

"It's too horrible to think of . . . and the worst of it is, he's *out with them now*. At this very moment, they could be . . . lying in wait for someone, attacking him even . . ."

"Steady," Gideon said. "There's no point in torturing yourself—"

He broke off as the telephone rang.

Marjorie went downstairs to answer it; and a moment later, was calling out, "Mr. Gideon! It's for you."

Gideon started. How could it be? Only Riddell knew he was here, and he had gone on to the meeting.

But it *was* Riddell. A tense, bitter Riddell who had been called back to the police station within a minute of leaving Gideon.

"It's the old, old Wellesley story. A man started off for the meeting in one of the quieter roads on the edge of the Estate. A hundred yards from his own doorstep, six youths wearing stocking masks jumped out from the shadows and attacked him. They coshed him, took his wallet and, just for kicks, made deep razor slashes all over his clothes. It's a miracle they didn't open up his chest or stomach. A patrol car found him lying in the gutter."

"How is he now?"

"Shaken up, slightly concussed perhaps, but otherwise okay. He's here at the station; I've been talking to him. A quieter, more inoffensive member of the public you couldn't imagine. As a matter of fact, he's a master at Wellesley High School. Got an absurdly grand name, because his parents called him after a poet, Gerard Manley Hopkins . . ."

Gideon started. The scrawl on an exercise book flashed across his mind, every dot and curl of the writing standing out as clearly as if it lay before him. *"Disgraceful work. See me. G.M.H."*

He had thought that message funny when he had first seen it: a welcome touch of the cozily normal. But here on the Wellesley Estate, even the cozily normal could have frighteningly abnormal consequences.

Sometimes a master in a bad temper would scrawl "See me" on a whole lot of exercise books in a single batch. Supposing Eric and his friends had all received the same irate summons . . . and had decided to answer it in their own way?

6

Alive or Dead?

COLDLY, FURIOUSLY ANGRY, Gideon asked Riddell to send the highest ranking plainclothesman at the substation over to the Beresford home, to wait for Eric and take him in for questioning. As an afterthought, he suggested that a plainclothes policewoman should come too, partly to soften the cold mechanics of arrest, partly to ensure that Marjorie was all right.

"Incidentally," he barked, "you'd better make sure that a police car isn't used. A Panda standing outside the house would be as good as a beacon warning Eric what he's in for when he gets home. Tell 'em to walk here as I did. Yes—*walk*. Half the trouble with policemen today is that they've forgotten they've got feet."

GIDEON HIMSELF HAD forgotten something. A policeman walking through a crowded estate at night was only inconspicuous as long as he didn't happen to be George Gideon, the best-known figure in the force.

His own walk to Marjorie Beresford's house, a quarter of an hour earlier, had been noticed by dozens of pairs of eyes; and those eyes were ready and waiting to observe the arrival of the CID team and Gideon's subsequent departure for the police station.

Eric may not have known what was in store for him on his return; but others knew and were grimly debating whether to let him arrive home at all.

GIDEON REACHED THE police station a prey to a pileup of conflicting pressures. It was eight-fifty-two. That meant that the meeting had already been in progress for twenty minutes or more. Angry audiences insisted on punctuality; unanimous ones didn't waste time. A vote on forming a vigilante force could be taken at any minute now; and once that vote had been passed, it would be too late for effective intervention, by himself or anyone else.

But it was here, not at the meeting, that the breaks were coming; and Gideon, a policeman first and a politician a long way second, simply could not force himself away.

Not, at any rate, until he had asked the strangely named Gerard Manley Hopkins just a few questions.

Riddell, he was told by the ever-plump sergeant, was talking to Hopkins in the interview room. Gideon grunted his thanks and walked straight in.

He found an odd conversation going on, not, he thought wryly, so much an interview as a brainstorming session.

"I'll tell you who the enemy is on this Estate, Superintendent. Society! A society that robs its young of all idealism, all dreams, all hope. That sets before them only the drab ambitions of a sick materialism—"

The speaker was a small, mild-eyed, prematurely white-haired man of about thirty-five. He was sitting forward in a plain wooden chair, a full cup of tea in his hand. He seemed to be as little aware of his circumstances as he was of the tea. Not once did his eyes stray down to the front of his pin-striped suit, even though it had been slashed into shreds. Around his midriff, the razor had cut through jacket, trousers, shirt and vest, leaving a square of flesh incongruously exposed.

Here we go again, Gideon thought wearily, how often have I heard this claptrap thundered out before? He decided it was time to intervene.

"Good evening, Mr. Hopkins. I'm Gideon, commander of the CID."

Hopkins rose from his chair, the forgotten teacup spilling its contents impartially over Gideon and himself.

"Oh, good lord! I really am sorry—"

"Don't worry." Gideon flicked a handkerchief over a saturated cuff. "I

56

have come to say how sorry I am about what's happened and to ask how you're feeling now."

"That's very civil of you, commander. I have a slight headache and feel a little confused, but—"

"Your memory of the attack is clear?"

"Oh, perfectly. I was just at the end of my road—Naughton Avenue—when five or six young men in stocking masks—"

So far, Gideon's manner had been gently purposeful. Now it subtly changed.

"Young men? Are you sure they weren't too young to be called that?"

Hopkins raised a hand, and gingerly touched the bruise at the back of his head where the cosh had landed.

"You mean, were they boys? It's possible, I suppose. Their faces were masked, as I say, and in the dark . . ."

Gideon stepped forward until he was almost standing over the little schoolmaster.

"Think back, Mr. Hopkins. Think back very carefully. Did you, even for a moment, find anything *familiar* about your attackers? In the way they moved, or perhaps spoke?"

Hopkins stared back as blankly as though he'd just been struck by the cosh again.

"I wish I knew what you were driving at, commander."

"Then I'll tell you," Gideon said crisply. He simply hadn't the time for more finesse. "I have reason to suspect that you might have been attacked by a boy called Eric Beresford and perhaps some of his friends in Form IIIB."

Hopkins' mouth opened with astonishment; but the astonishment didn't reach his eyes, which registered an extraordinary procession of emotions—shock, horror, consternation, and then sadness and pity.

Pity! Gideon nearly choked. That this little man could sit here, his body aching all over from a savage, uncalled-for attack, his clothes virtually falling off him because of a vicious razoring, and feel *pity* . . .

"I very much hope your suspicions are unfounded, commander," Hopkins said, in a voice that suggested that his hopes were at variance with his belief. "But, in any case, you can't expect me to do anything to confirm them. These boys you mention are my pupils, my charges. I am myself

57

therefore a part of the social environment that has thwarted, enraged, betrayed them. It is my business—it is the business of all of us—to try to *understand* . . ."

Gideon took a long, deep breath.

"You wouldn't, I trust, take understanding to the point of withholding information from the police?"

"Naturally not, Commander."

"Then perhaps you would be kind enough to do me one small favor. I believe you wrote 'Disgraceful work. See me' in a number of boys' exercise books last week."

"Ah, yes. Some really appalling essays were turned in at the start of the new term."

"Do you think you could make me a list of the boys who earned that note on their exercise books?"

"It will be difficult, but I will certainly try."

"Take your time," Gideon said. "I'll get a sergeant to come in, and you can dictate the list to him, when you're ready. After that, if you're feeling up to it, he'll drive you home."

The schoolmaster smiled at last.

"Home. Yes. I'll be glad to get there. My wife, Charlotte . . . she's a great worrier, you know. So's my daughter, Karen, even though she's only five. They know my sense of duty is always stirred by the underprivileged."

Gideon's private view that the underprivileged had now become the over-privileged he kept to himself. He gestured to Riddell, and the two men went out together, feeling equally dazed and beaten at the havoc do-gooders could wreak.

They were halfway down the corridor when they heard a crash behind them and turned back.

Perhaps as an aftereffect of the coshing, perhaps because of what he had just realized about his pupils, Gerard Manley Hopkins had slithered off the wooden chair and was lying in a dead faint on the interview-room floor.

GIDEON STAYED ONLY long enough to reassure himself that Hopkins's heart was beating strongly and that he would recover soon. Then, briskly ordering the sergeant to take over, he strode out of the station and started to walk the fifty yards to the community center. He walked quickly, giving little thought to Riddell, who had his work cut out to keep up with him.

"Ten past nine," Gideon grunted, by way of explanation for his haste. "We could have lost, Tom. They could easily have taken that vigilante vote by now."

But no. Mr. Harold Neame, the headmaster of Wellesley High School, was a prosy man. He had only just reached his peroration when Gideon and Riddell arrived at the hall.

It was a peroration that they would have preferred to miss.

Coldly, implacably, Neame itemized the failures of the police in their area: their failure to stop the endless muggings; their failure to arrest a significant number of suspects; their failure to idenitfy and expose the source of the outrages; above all, their failure to keep law and order.

Neame was a very different type of schoolmaster from Gerard Hopkins. A tall, donnish-looking man in his late fifties, he had thin, academic features and long, straggly hair, which he brushed continually from his eyes. The eyes themselves were cold and hawklike, matching his chilling manner.

Despite this manner, perhaps because of it, Neame was rousing high emotion in his audience. At the end of every sentence of his indictment of the police, there were thunderous growls of agreement. Gideon and Riddell, pushing their way through the jam-packed hall, felt that every one of those growls was a direct accusation aimed at themselves.

Neame suddenly made sure of it.

He broke off to point a long, bony forefinger directly at them.

"I am delighted to see that Commander Gideon, head of the CID and, through television, a familiar figure to everyone in Britain, has decided to honor us with his presence. I am also pleased to welcome Chief Detective Superintendent Riddell, who, I understand, has been in charge of the police investigations here throughout the past weeks. I do not think that any of us need be surprised that these gentlemen are arriving when our meeting is almost over. Everything the police have done in Wellesley has been characterized by a certain . . . slowness off the mark . . . shall we say?"

This was greeted by a roar of laughter that threatened to split Gideon's eardrums. He had reached his seat now, vacated by one of the plain-clothesmen, but did not sit down. Arms folded, jaw thrust out, he stood there, easily the most commanding figure in the room, waiting for the sound of ironic hilarity to die down.

But the roar didn't die down. It changed its note, became a vocal tidal wave of derision and disgust. Torches, walkingsticks, newspapers, clenched fists were being waved at him from all sides; and behind them, beneath them, were now row after row of angry, frightened faces.

It was like a nightmare: the worst nightmare of his life.

Beside him, Gideon heard Riddell breathing hard, and wondered how far he was from breaking point. He became aware of other things: the unwinking eyes of TV news cameras, taking this painful moment of police history to the nation, to the world. A crowd of suspiciously well-dressed youths occupying the rows of seats immediately behind him. What were they here for? To cause trouble, start a fight? Suddenly he spotted a familiar face in the middle of them: John Rowlandes, old Malcolm's son, the DC from the area patrol car. Gideon's spirits rose at the sight of him. So his little ploy had succeeded; the derided police had one man planted in the midst of the enemy . . .

The demonstration was beginning to subside at last. Probably it was Gideon's expression that was doing it. He managed to look as totally unmoved as a rock being hit by a schoolboy's pebbles.

As soon as individual voices could be heard again, Harold Neame shouted from the platform.

"I do not think I need say anything further to express the feelings of this meeting. But while Mr. Gideon is on his feet I would like to ask him one question. Can he deny that in the circumstances in which the Wellesley Estate finds itself today, the only sensible, honorable course for its citizens to take is to found a law-keeping force of their own?"

A total silence descended on the room, as everyone waited for Gideon's reply.

This was his moment, Gideon told himself. Everything would be lost if he muffed it.

Loudly and clearly his voice boomed through the hall.

"I wouldn't dream of denying it, Mr. Neame. I've come here to propose exactly the same thing myself."

THERE WAS ANOTHER silence, this time a stunned one.

Neame, as thoroughly taken aback as his audience, brushed gray strands of hair out of his eyes.

"Did I hear you correctly, Mr. Gideon? You say you have come here to propose setting up a vigilante force?"

"That is so," Gideon said easily, "but not quite the force you're probably thinking of. I had a long consultation with the commissioner of the metropolitan police this afternoon. I put it to him—and he agreed with me—that there was a strong case here in Wellesley for setting up something completely new in the history of crime prevention: a police-directed army of part-time volunteers, a sort of home guard against crime. They would be identified by special armbands and patrol the Estate in groups of six to eight. A smaller group would not give effective enough protection. Each unit would keep in constant walkie-talkie touch with a central control point, probably the police substation—"

A feeling of excitement was sweeping through the room. This audience of furious malcontents was beginning to reveal itself for what it really was: a collection of normal citizens suffering from a combination of fear and frustration. Gideon's calmness eased their fears: the clarity and detail of his proposals sliced through their frustration. What they needed was a clear-cut plan of action, involving every man and woman who wished to volunteer; a plan that was ready to be put into immediate effect; and that was exactly what George Gideon was giving them.

Even Neame's attitude was changing. When he spoke again, the cold anger had gone from his voice. In its place was something very like respect.

"Would these patrolling units have the power to arrest?"

"Certainly," Gideon said. "And it wouldn't take any special legislation to give it to them. Every citizen has the right to arrest anyone whom he sees breaking the law. These volunteers would simply be acting on their ancient basic rights as citizens. Of course, they wouldn't be able to search houses or hold suspects for questioning . . . but, as I've said, they'll be in direct radio touch with the police, and a Panda car can reach any part of the Estate in under two minutes. So they shouldn't be by any means powerless in any situation."

"How soon can this force be started?" someone asked.

"If enough of you come forward at the end of this meeting, there's no reason why the first patrols shouldn't be out tonight."

There were excited murmurs, gasps of astonishment, grunts of approval. This was the kind of talk they had come to hear all right; and they had got more of it in two minutes from Gideon than in nearly three-quarters of an hour of listening to Harold Neame.

"What shall we call this force?" asked a cheerful, red-faced woman farther along Gideon's row. "The Gideonites?"

The roar of laughter that followed was warm, enthusiastic, anything but mocking.

"I don't care what we call it," Gideon replied, "as long as it brings the walls of violence tumbling down."

This was greeted by actual applause, in which one man—a sour, dyspeptic looking individual in the front row—definitely did not join.

He got to his feet and shouted, contemptuously, "Shakespeare was right about the many-headed multitude! Five minutes ago you were all attacking the police for their bungling incompetence. Now you want them to take charge of this whole vigilante project. Why? Do you want to have *that* bungled too?"

Gideon turned red with fury. But his voice remained calm, deliberate, matter-of-fact.

"If I believed there had been a single moment of incompetence in the handling of this inquiry," he said, "I would not be here to defend it. And the chief detective superintendent in charge of the case would not be standing here beside me. The plain truth is that in any free community, the police are only as strong as the public's will to support them. For reasons that I won't go into now, public support for the police on this Estate has become dangerously weak. If, as I hope and believe, this meeting marks a dramatic change in that situation, then I can make you this promise. With your help, the violence on the Wellesley Estate can be ended, once and for all, in a matter of *days* from now!"

It was perhaps the rashest promise of his life. And he had made it in front of TV cameras and half the crime reporters of Fleet Street. If he failed to fulfill it, it could mean nothing less than the end of his career. Yet Gideon felt no twinge of anxiety; only confidence that he had spoken the literal truth.

And if he was wrong—if he had really put his head on the block—at least there was one consolation. As far as this meeting was concerned, he had won an overwhelming victory. A good half of the people in the hall were on their feet cheering. Harold Neame, his expression of sour denunciation now turned to approval, was clapping lustily: as was the supporting committee on the platform behind him. All along Gideon's row, people were pressing forward to talk to him, smiling, waving, wanting him and Riddell to shake their hands.

But in the row *behind* Gideon, there was a different story.

The well-dressed youths were looking around them with silent, vicious anger.

Gideon heard a sudden whisper.

"Let's stick the pigs!"

He whirled around, in time to see chairs crashing over, fists flailing, the sharp gleam of a razor blade . . .

The trouble didn't last long. The constables at the door, and the plain-clothesmen who had been positioned all over the audience, had had their eyes on those youths from the beginning of the meeting and were more than ready. But it took them a few moments to get across the hall and close in.

And it was during those moments that a very strange event took place.

John Rowlandes got to his feet, kicked over his chair, pushed past two or three of his fellow troublemakers, and arrived immediately behind Gideon.

And as Gideon swung around toward him, he aimed a right hook at the commander's jaw.

The blow didn't connect: it was obvious that Rowlandes hadn't intended it to. But the force of it brought the young PDC lurching forward, and for a second his lips were less than an inch from Gideon's ear.

"Hit back, sir. It'll put me in good with this mob, see?"

Gideon only just stopped himself from a very sharp retort. For a commander to be ordered to take a certain course of action by a green-as-grass detective constable was startling enough. What was even more startling was the realization that the cool young Rowlandes was absolutely right.

By aiming that single blow at Gideon, he had almost certainly made himself the hero of the night with the yobs. But there was just a chance that one of them would have spotted how wide of the mark the blow had fallen; would suspect a trick.

If he, the august Gideon, were to hit back with a real blow . . .

63

Gideon grinned inwardly.

"Right, young feller-me-lad," he muttered, under his breath. "You've asked for it. You'll get it."

Totally unmindful of the TV cameras, the watching crowd, the effect on the Gideon image if he indulged in public brawling, he delivered a swift uppercut direct to the young DC's jaw.

Rowlandes dropped like a stone and lay still.

The group of youths gasped. The air became blue with some of the choicest language Gideon had ever heard. But that wasn't entirely because of what had happened to Rowlandes. The constables were arriving in the rebels' row, with plainclothesmen hard behind them. They were picking out the biggest troublemakers and marching them off. Gideon heard that old, old phrase "are you coming quietly?" repeated again and again.

Amidst all the confusion, Rowlandes lay white and still.

Gideon clambered over the back of his seat and knelt down beside him. He had judged that blow very carefully, to put Rowlandes down for a count of eight or nine. But twenty seconds at least had passed since the blow.

Was he feigning unconsciousness, building up the drama? Or had something gone wrong? Had he cracked his head against the edge of a seat in going down, or—

One thing became certain as Gideon looked closer at his young protégé; and the realization of it made his blood turn to ice as he leaned forward and gently felt for Rowlandes's pulse.

There could be no faking about that gaping mouth, those open, sightless eyes. It wasn't a question of whether he was conscious or unconscious; it was a question of whether he was alive or dead.

IN TWO OTHER parts of London, at almost exactly the same moment, almost identical questions were being asked.

Two hundred and fifty yards across the Wellesley Estate, Marjorie Beresford heard a sound outside her front door. It was a terrible sound, halfway between a cry of "Mum" and a moan of agony.

She raced the detective inspector and the policewoman to the door and was the first to see Eric lying half on, half off the doorstep. The light there wasn't good; the bulb in the porch had been smashed by vandals weeks before and had never been replaced. But there was enough illumination to show that Eric's shirt front was covered with blood, and there was no doubting this time that the blood was his own.

Marjorie tried to bend forward, but her strength gave out, and she fell to the ground, taking with her into oblivion the most terrifying question of her life: was Eric, her son, alive or dead?

SIX MILES AWAY to the north, in Finchley, Dino Orisini had just closed his restaurant for the night.

He and his wife, Vittoria, were standing over the till. Dino had no head for figures, and it was usually Vittoria who counted the night's takings.

He hoped she wouldn't notice that every note and coin he handled became wet with the sweat of fear that was dampening his fingers. He wished he could silence the panicky questions that throbbed so persistently inside his skull.

Would this be the last time that he and Vittoria worked together? Did *anything* together?

Who could say how soon Rocco's hatchetmen would get busy, once he had gone to that Soho pub and thrown down the gauntlet to the gang?

This time tomorrow, would he be alive or dead?

IN ONE PART of London, the question was not being asked, but answered.

Inside that strange, near-derelict house in Dulwich, Gordon Cargill and Matt Honiwell had been sitting in eerie silence for more than an hour. During all that time, Jacob Brodnik—a frail, quiet-voiced man with a strangely commanding manner—had been lost in a trancelike reverie.

He had asked them not to disturb him, and they hadn't, even though the tension had risen to near breaking point inside each of them.

Now, at last, it seemed that their vigil was over.

Jacob Brodnik suddenly, with a shuddering sigh, rose from his shabby armchair.

"I have good news for you, Mr. Cargill. Your wife is alive. Though the signals I am getting are so faint that I fear I must add—'just.'" Brodnik's voice became stronger, every word carrying a mysterious authority. "There is, however, no need to be alarmed. With the full cooperation of the

65

police—such as I was given in Holland over the Van Este affair last March—I am absolutely confident that she can be traced in time."

Matt Honiwell had trouble finding his voice.

"Wh-what exactly, Mr. Brodnik, would this full cooperation entail?"

Brodnik shrugged.

"A hundred, perhaps two hundred, men carrying out my instructions without question for a space of, perhaps, forty-eight hours."

Matt groaned aloud.

Gideon's words rang in his head, as clearly as though George were in the room.

"No matter what the Belgians or the Dutch may do, I simply can't allow the valuable time of valuable men to be expended on ESP wild-goose chases . . ."

Equally clearly, Matt remembered his own indignant rejoinder.

"Do you really think I'd ask you to?"

After such an exchange it was going to be impossible to detail even one man, let alone two hundred, to carry out Mr. Brodnik's instructions.

But Gordon Cargill's eyes were shining with the first glint of hope that they had shown during all these weary weeks.

And—for the moment, at least—Matt Honiwell could not bring himself to say, "That's impossible."

7

Blood Lust

GIDEON'S EAR WAS less than an inch from John Rowlandes's mouth when he first detected the faint sound of breathing. Hope, tremulous at first, began to burgeon in his mind, turning into a roaring torrent of relief as each breath became stronger. Suddenly the young DC gulped, blinked, and tried to sit up.

"Easy," Gideon said. "East does it . . ."

He noticed a bruise, red but already beginning to blacken, close to Rowlandes's left temple. So that was it: he had caught his head a glancing blow against a chair on the way down.

Already, he wasn't looking too much the worse for it. He was grinning shakily; but if there was a slight risk of concussion, there was a much stronger one that he might momentarily forget his role as a teenage tough and revert to behaving as a DC.

Most of his fellow toughs had been marched away by this time; but one or two, the ones who had not actually been violent, were still around and within earshot.

For their benefit, Gideon stood up abruptly and roared: "Right. Get this young hooligan out of here, feet first. I want an ambulance at once, make-shift if necessary, to take him to the hospital. The doctor there ought to run an eye over him—"

Two burly constables came forward; one seized Rowlandes under the arms, and the other took his ankles. Rowlandes suddenly remembered his role, that is, if he'd ever forgotten it. He put on a great show of struggling to escape and snarled at Gideon.

"Do you really think you've made a hospital case out of me, king pig? Give me half a chance and I'll make one out of *you* . . ."

"You've had all the chances you'll be getting for today—and for many days to come, if you don't behave yourself," Gideon answered curtly. "Take him away. Either to the hospital or a police station cell. The choice is his. But that's the only choice he's getting."

Exhausted with his brief bout of histrionic defiance, Rowlandes allowed himself to be carried out. Various hostile murmurs told Gideon that some members of the audience, probably women with strong maternal instincts, were turning against him again. No doubt he had sounded like a bully. Balancing this were other murmurs, probably from men, which sounded like grunts of approval for his toughness. That man had been right to call the crowd a "many-headed multitude." Out of the corner of his eye, Gideon noticed that the TV cameras at the back of the hall were still focused on him. Anything and everything he did was liable to be shown on television before the evening was out. They already had his original punch-up in the can. But then, they also had his impassioned speech for public support for the police and his carefully thought-out proposals for a police-directed vigilante "home guard." Which Gideon image would be projected across the nation? The forceful leader or the apparently irresponsible brawler? It would be for the backroom boys, the television news editors, to decide, and Gideon needed no telling which would be considered the more sensational.

Still, it was too late to worry about that now. The important thing was to see that John Rowlandes had the maximum opportunity to capitalize on the incident.

Gideon took Riddell aside, well out of the hearing of the remaining toughs, well out of range of those probing TV lenses.

"Tom, can you get a message through to the hospital? Ask them, as a favor to the police, to keep Rowlandes under observation for at least forty-eight hours." He corrected himself. "On second thoughts—make that as a personal favor to *me*. I know most of the staff there. I think they'll play ball."

"What's the idea, George?"

Gideon prayed silently for tolerance. Riddell wasn't usually as thick-headed as this. One had to remember how much this case was telling on him; what strain he was under the whole time.

He explained as patiently as he could.

"If the word goes out that Rowlandes has been put into the hospital because of a fracas with me, he'll be more of a hero to that mob than ever. Then, if I drop all charges against him, and the police keep clear, it's a virtual certainty that he'll get visits from members of the gang. It's quite possible he'll get an admiring crowd of them around his bed. And from such visits he might pick up a very great deal."

Riddell suddenly woke up and started thinking very fast—almost faster than Gideon.

"You're right there. We must make sure he's booked in under an assumed name. And we'll have to give him a fake identity—one that will hold up, however closely the gang checks." His imagination started working overtime. "How about Frank 'Fingers' Fenton, a dangerous young criminal, just out of Pentonville Prison after a two-year stretch for armed robbery? He could have been lodging on the Estate with an old aunt. I know just the woman who'll play the part of aunt for us—she lives in—"

Gideon grinned delightedly.

"Now you're talking. Could you get all that laid on?"

"In two minutes, George. I'll be right back."

Riddell, suddenly confident again, headed for the doorway. Gideon watched his purposeful progress with a thoughtful sigh. If only Tom were always like this—

His reverie was interrupted. Harold Neame was back on the platform, calling the meeting to order in his most headmasterly style.

"Ladies and gentlemen," he thundered, and might almost have been saying, "Wake up at the back there!" to the fifth form. "I must apologize for this interrupted meeting, but perhaps the interruption has served a purpose. It has brought us face to face with the ugly violence in our midst and should strengthen our determination to take immediate and urgent action against it. May I remind you that, just before the uproar started, Commander Gideon was suggesting that if sufficient volunteers came forward, the first vigilante patrol could go out tonight. That was what you said, wasn't it, Mr. Gideon?"

Gideon stood up, aware that once again, all eyes—and both TV cameras—were on him.

"That was what I said," he stated flatly, "and that was what I meant."

There was a tap on his arm. He tried to ignore it, but the pressure increased. He turned impatiently, and saw that Riddell was back. That grab—and a certain wildness in his eye—told him that Riddell's inner tension was building up again; but he was struggling hard against it, and his voice was surprisingly calm as he said:

"Sorry to break in, George, but something's happened you should know about. The inspector at the Beresford house—his name's Dunne—has just rung through. Mrs. Beresford went to the front door after hearing a cry—and found Eric lying on the doorstep with a knife in his chest."

Gideon's exasperation gave way to a deep, cold dread.

"Is the boy—"

"Dead? No, not quite. But he hasn't much chance, I gather. The knife went in a tenth of an inch from the heart. They've had the ambulance there already. He could be at the hospital by now."

"And Marj—Mrs. Beresford? How's she taking it?"

"I gather she went out like a light."

"Best thing. Is she still unconscious?"

"I should say not. There were sobs and screams in the background over the telephone. The doctor didn't stop to give her a sedative—he was too busy dealing with Eric—"

"Yes. Yes, I can imagine." Marjorie Beresford's delicate, plain little face flashed in front of Gideon's eyes. How many more times in her life would that poor woman be called upon to bear the unbearable?

"Has Dunne rung off now?" he asked.

"No. He's hanging on in case you want to speak to him."

"Right. Then I'll come."

Gideon glanced around. The whole hall had become deathly quiet. Probably very few of the people in the audience had managed to catch more than a word or two of this whispered consultation, but Gideon's and Riddell's expression had told them, clearly enough, that some shocking incident had taken place.

They might as well know the worst, Gideon thought. It had never been his policy to keep information from the public unnecessarily.

"Ladies and gentlemen," he announced. "I have just heard that there has been a stabbing on the Estate, perhaps a fatal one, involving a thirteen-year-old boy. Please excuse me for a few minutes."

He turned and strode out of the hall. Behind him, he heard people bombarding Riddell with questions. He caught neither the questions nor Riddell's answers. All he could think of was Marjorie Beresford at the end of her endurance.

A respectful constable led him into the foyer. The telephone was in a cubicle that functioned as a box office for the community center. The inside was festooned with torn and dusty posters advertising discos and bingo sessions. All the dates on the posters were two months back; all had "Canceled" slips posted across them, painful reminders of how long terror had reigned in Wellesley, how much time had passed since normal life had been possible here.

Gideon picked up the telephone, and a moment later Detective Inspector Dunne was giving him full details of what had happened at the Beresfords'. Only one new fact emerged. A trail of blood had been found leading from the gate to the doorstep. Either the stabbing had taken place on the pavement, or, more probably, the boy had been knifed in a car and then dumped at the gate. Somehow he had managed to crawl the last few yards home.

Suddenly the sobbing was there in the background again.

"That's Mrs. Beresford, sir, she's . . . a little bit distraught," Dunne said, in patient explanation.

"So would you be, if you'd been through half what she has," Gideon said sharply. "Is Sergeant Baker there? If so, put her on."

Sergeant Baker—a young and rather pretty policewoman—came on the line. It appeared that Mrs. Beresford was demanding to be allowed to go to the hospital to be close to her son.

"Well, there's no law against that, is there?"

"No, sir, but she's recently been in a dead faint and is now on the verge of hysteria. In these circumstances, I don't think it wise to let her go just yet. Of course, if you feel differently . . ."

Gideon grunted. He couldn't deny that the girl was probably right. What Marjorie desperately needed was the comfort and company of someone she knew. Someone with a strong yet gentle personality who would keep her calm; accompany her to the hospital if she so desperately wanted to go; and see her through whatever happened to her son.

It seemed an impossible problem, but the answer, when it came, was so simple that it stunned him.

Kate would go like a shot. And she'd be perfect.

What's more, she'd never forgive him if he denied her the chance of doing all she could for a friend in such desperate distress.

Within seconds, Gideon had rung Kate and explained. For a moment, she was speechless with shock at the news; then her only concern was to get to Marjorie as soon as possible. Gideon arranged for a police car to rush her to the Beresford house. The car would stand by to take her and Marjorie to the hospital, if required. It would be best to leave it to Kate to decide whether or not Marjorie was in a fit state to go.

Gideon was on the point of telephoning the hospital to get a report on Eric's condition, when he was stopped by the sound of angry shouting coming from the hall behind him.

He hurried out of the kiosk and made for the swing doors leading to the auditorium. Just as he reached them, he hesitated, some instinct telling him to pause and size up the situation before entering the hall. The doors had two rectangular pieces of glass in them, crisscrossed by wires as a protection against vandalism; nevertheless it was possible to see through it.

He could easily make out the bulky figure of Tom Riddell, still on his feet, and struggling to make himself heard. Gideon opened the door an inch, and could just make out Riddell's words above the din.

"All I am proposing is that you should wait for Commander Gideon's return before talking any more about sending out patrols tonight. This knifing has changed the situation drastically. We do not know what further mischief may be planned. There could be other cases of murderous violence, which might erupt anywhere in Wellesley. In the circumstances, to allow small bands of unarmed, untrained civilian volunteers to roam the Estate all night would be like sending lambs to the slaughter. I feel—"

72

The rest of his words were lost in a roar of fury. Gideon let the door swing shut again, stood back, and leaned heavily against a wall. That bloody fool Riddell! Certainly, he was going by the copper's rule book—the policeman's first duty was to see that citizens were never unnecessarily put at risk—but rule books didn't help against a hostile populace in a lynch-mob mood. With great difficulty he, Gideon, had damped down that mood by promising instant action in which the public could be directly involved. By virtually withdrawing that promise on the first provocation, Riddell was making it look as though the police weren't serious—had, in fact, got cold feet about the whole vigilante scheme.

Gideon almost groaned aloud. The psychological damage that had been done might be very hard to repair.

Just how hard became all too clear a moment later.

The shouting stopped—or, rather, thinned into a single shouting voice. Gideon stepped back to the door and saw through the glass that someone from the hall—the sour, dyspeptic-looking man who had called the audience a "many-headed multitude" earlier on—had jumped onto the platform beside Neame, and was making a speech of almost Hitler-like savagery.

Gideon didn't have to open the door to hear him. The thin, strident voice, pitched on a note of high hysteria, pierced glass and wood with ease.

"So murderous violence is being planned against us, is it? In that case, ladies and gentlemen, I suggest there is only one answer—to get murderously violent ourselves. Let's all go out of this hall together—a great, irresistible army—and not stop until we've hounded every hooligan off the Estate. We must search every street, every garden, every house, every *room,* even. And each time we find a boy with a knife, or a razor, or a gun, or so much as a guilty look, we'll . . ."

For a moment, Gideon thought the man was actually going to say "string him up." But, perhaps mindful of the TV cameras, he ended less wildly, ". . . give him a taste of his own medicine." It came to the same thing, of course, Gideon thought grimly. That phrase could be a license for anything—kicking, beating, knifing—total bloodlust in the name of justice. And if the hooligans ganged up and replied in kind, tonight could be one of the bloodiest ever experienced in Britain in time of peace.

It had to be stopped—and stopped immediately.

But *how?*

8

Lambs to the Slaughter?

THE PEOPLE IN the hall were clapping their approval. Or, at least, some of them were. From the rather thin volume of sound, Gideon sensed that quite a few members of the audience must be refraining from joining in; and even Neame and the platform committee (or, at least, as many members of them as he could see through the narrow pane) were looking hesitant, clearly in two minds about how far they wanted to go.

If he could walk in there and somehow, very quickly, restore the confidence in the police that Riddell had destroyed, there might still—just—be a chance of saving the day.

Once Gideon saw what he had to do, he hesitated less than a second before starting to do it. He strode straight through the swing doors, making sure that they swung to behind him, with a resounding enough *thud* to turn half the heads in the audience his way. He strode on down the main aisle, looking neither right nor left until he reached the platform. He did not bother to climb the steps. His commanding personality, coupled with his height and bulk, enabled him to dominate the hall quite effortlessly from where he was.

Neame, the passionate orator, the committee—all on the platform were overshadowed as effectively as though a bright spotlight had swung away from them.

"I'm sorry I was so long," Gideon said briskly. "There were several matters in connection with the knifing incident that required to be dealt with urgently." He gave the impression that he was totally unaware that anything of importance had happened since he had left the hall. What was more, by some magic of the will, he succeeded in suggesting that nothing important *could* have happened while he'd been away.

"Incidentally," he continued, very firmly and confidently, "I have had clearer thoughts about tonight's vigilante patrols. Now that this violence has taken place, they will be more urgently needed than ever. And I don't think we should wait until this meeting is over; I think we should send them out at once." It was a temptation to glance at Riddell, but Gideon resisted it. His voice sharpened as incisively as if he were giving a Yard briefing.

"It is now ten o'clock. If we're quick, we could get the first patrols on the streets by ten-thirty. It will take two patrols, with six members in each, to patrol the Estate adequately; and we ought to have it patrolled until well after daybreak—say six-thirty A.M. tomorrow. So I suggest we have two further patrols ready to take over from the first ones halfway through the night, at two-thirty A.M. That means I require twenty-four volunteers for tonight's patrolling and thirty-six for tomorrow night, when we'll be having three shifts starting at eight P.M. In other words, I'm appealing for sixty of you to volunteer. *Now.*"

There was a long, agonizing pause. Then Neame, on the platform, said authoritatively, "Count me in, commander, as number one."

He left the platform, the entire vigilante committee following him to "sign on." Gideon took down their names in a notebook, not batting an eyelid as he listed two clergymen, an engine driver, and a chiropodist among them. Then the speaker's table was pressed into service as a recruiting officer's desk, and Gideon detailed two uniformed constables to sit there and take the rest of the names. The Hitler-like demagogue disappeared somewhere behind the queue that was forming three deep down the central aisle. His speech had been forgotten as completely as if he had never made it. Instead of a hysterical invitation to a combined witch-hunt and bloodbath, the public felt that it had been offered a sensible, practical job to do. And it was jumping at the chance.

Within a quarter of an hour, the sixty volunteers had signed on; and then Harold Neame proposed that the meeting should close.

76

"Commander Gideon has promised that, as far as it's humanly possible, this action will be enough to end the violence on this Estate," he said. "I suggest we take him at his word and hold no more meetings until we have had a chance to see the effect of—Gideon's Force."

Without realizing it, the donnish headmaster had coined the name that was to stay with the new organization from that moment forward.

The motion was carried *nem con*; the meeting broke up; the TV men started dismantling their lights and cameras, preparing to go home.

The sixty volunteers remained, waiting for instructions.

Gideon didn't keep them waiting long.

"I am afraid I am going to have to ask all of you to accompany me to the station," he announced sternly; then added, with a grin: "It is only fifty yards down the road. It will be easier there to work out the rotas for the different patrols; to issue patrol leaders with walkie-talkies, and so on. Would you all please follow me, and we'll decide which of you are to be sent out on patrol duty straight away. I hope we shan't detain you long."

A minute later, Gideon was striding down the street toward the station with Riddell at his side, the crowd of volunteer vigilantes, led by Harold Neame and his committee, closely following.

Neame was leading in a typical headmaster's style, his forward stride being one of absolute confidence. Behind him came the committee and, behind them, the rest of the volunteers—a mixed assortment of human types, mostly men, but with a fair sprinkling of women. A wealthy-looking middle-aged woman walked side by side with an Irish youth in a bus conductor's uniform. An attractive girl in jeans walked arm in arm with a senior citizen, dressed in what looked like a wartime air warden's suit. Gideon, who had asked all the volunteers to list their occupations along with their names and addresses, knew that among this throng were bank clerks, shop assistants, draughtsmen, factory workers, nurses, TV repairers, hairdressers, teachers, housewives, milkmen—in fact, people in almost every job one could think of. A complete cross section of the Wellesley Estate was walking behind him; with only a little exaggeration, one could call it a complete cross section of Britain.

The grimness with which everyone had walked toward the hall earlier that evening had entirely disappeared. There was a strong sense of excitement in the air, and most of the crowd were laughing and talking among themselves as gaily as though they were off on some holiday excursion. The committee tried to hold themselves aloof, but even one or two of them were grinning.

Only Tom Riddell remained grim. Since Gideon's intervention he hadn't spoken once, and his face, or as much of it as Gideon could see in the darkness, was white and haunted. Perhaps he was remembering his disastrous speech and how close it had brought the whole Estate to the brink of a holocaust. Or perhaps he still had reservations about the idea of using civilian patrols.

This second guess proved to be the right one.

Riddell suddenly turned and said quietly, so that no one behind them could hear, "George. All this patrolling—is it just a device to keep the lynch-mob occupied, or do you really believe it can stop the violence?"

"I really believe it can stop the violence," Gideon answered. "And I'll tell you why. The last time the Estate had peace and quiet was when Uniform was doing its 'saturation policing.' They had so many men here that every point on the Estate was passed by a policeman—how frequently? You know the statistics better than I do."

"Every twelve to fourteen minutes," Riddell answered flatly, as though reciting from an overfamiliar textbook.

"Right," Gideon said. "Now, with two patrols making the whole Estate their beat from ten-thirty to six-thirty, supplemented by two area cars on constant patrol, we can actually beat that figure. Every point on the Estate should, by my reckoning, be passed either by a patrol or an area car every nine to eleven minutes. Nobody's pretending that that's a final answer to the violence. But it ought to damp it down for a while—and a few days' grace is all we should need to bring the ringleaders to book. I've a hunch we're pretty hot on their trail."

"*You* are, George, that's for certain. But isn't there a danger that, for that very reason, the violence will escalate rather than die down?" Riddell's voice suddenly became harsh and strident, betraying nerves that were taut as bowstrings. "For instance, do you know why I think Eric Beresford was knifed tonight? It was simply because *you* were seen coming and going from his house."

Gideon was so shaken that he stopped dead in the street, oblivious to the confusion this created behind him. The thought that he might inadvertently have *caused* what had happened to Eric was one of the biggest shocks in a

78

shattering night. He had a childish impulse to deny angrily that the evidence suggested any such thing. But he checked himself. He had to admit that Riddell's theory was not only feasible; it was almost the only tenable explanation. What other motive could the enemy have had for suddenly turning—murderously—on one of their own gang?

Gideon began walking again, now at a greatly increased pace.

"If you're right," he said, "and you certainly may be—this organization really must have eyes everywhere."

"They have, George, they *have!*" Under normal circumstances, Riddell would never have dreamed of addressing his superior, in such familiar terms, in a voice that could not fail to carry to listening ears. But the man was beyond such niceties: he was perilously close to being beyond reason. His obsessive fear and hatred of the mysterious evil on the Estate seemed to have taken over his entire personality, making him as unmanageable as a madman.

"And do you realize what this means?" he declared loudly, oblivious of the fact that by now the whole crowd was his audience. "The enemy will have detailed knowledge of this patrol operation from the word 'go.' No matter how hard we try to screen the volunteers, their spies will get in. No matter how frequently we change the rotas or the routes, they'll know where each patrol will be at any given time. And at some point, they're bound to plan an ambush—probably a quick knife attack by one of their most vicious mugging units. The patrol-leader will be pounced on first, his walkie-talkie snatched, before he's said a word. The first the control point at the station will know of the attack will be ten minutes later, when an area car goes past and sees the bodies of the patrol."

"The bodies of the patrol . . ."

The phrase had all the impact of a blow, and it sent Gideon's senses reeling as if he had been physically winded. Half of his mind was inclined to dismiss Riddell's fears as the product of a near-paranoic obsession; the other half whispered that they could be alarmingly close to the truth.

The volunteers evidently felt the same. No one in the crowd could have missed hearing Riddell's declaration, and it had had a dramatic effect. The excited laughing and chattering had given way to a tense, strained silence.

They were outside the police station now. Gideon slowly climbed the half-dozen steps that led to the main entrance, still unsure how to cope with the situation; what, if anything, to say. By the time he reached the top of the flight he had decided. It was only right to play it straight with these people—to tell them there was an outside chance that they had been listening to the truth.

He turned and faced them, his expression almost as grim as Riddell's. The police station's blue lamp, immediately above his head, made him seem, more than ever, a massive embodiment of British justice, British law.

"Ladies and gentlemen," he said. "I gather you've all heard my colleague's views on the risks you are facing. I assure you that the police will take every possible step to see that those risks are minimized. On the other hand, if Chief Detective Superintendent Riddell's assessment of the situation turns out to be correct, then obviously your lives will be in a certain amount of peril. If any—or all—of you wish to withdraw—"

"Withdraw?"

The word was flung back at him in a roar of derisive contempt.

"What do you take us for, Commander?" The speaker was the senior citizen in the air warden's suit. "I thought you said you were organizing a 'home guard' against crime. Well, I know something about the real Home Guard—I served as a sergeant in it, clean through World War II. And what d'you imagine my platoon would have thought of me if I'd said: 'Do you wish to withdraw tonight, lads? There might be a bit of an air raid.' Whatever the risks you're talking about, I don't reckon they're bigger than Hitler's bombs were, then."

"And quite apart from that," Neame was talking now, his thin, donnish tones in startling contrast to the ex-sergeant's rich Cockney, "what about the risks to our wives and children if we don't take a stand, once and for all, against the violence here?"

Gideon, for the moment, was lost for a reply. Over and over again, during his career, he had felt humbled by the courage and determination shown by policemen under his command. It was an odd experience to have the same feeling about a cross-section of the public—that public that had behaved like a mindless rabble only half an hour before.

It was a moment before he could trust his voice. Then he said, gruffly, "Well—if you're all agreed—in the station, everybody, please."

Watched by a despairing Riddell, the crowd surged forward toward the steps. At that moment—finally, irrevocably—Gideon's Force was born.

9

Halfway Up a Hill

AT THAT MOMENT, six miles away in West Dulwich, another kind of force was very definitely *not* being born: that force of a hundred or more policemen that Jacob Brodnik had requested should be put under his command—to, as he put it, "carry out my instructions without question for the space of forty-eight hours."

Gradually, in the course of a long, agonizing discussion, Matt Honiwell had been cornered into admitting that, as far as the Yard was concerned, such an arrangement was out of the question.

For all his frailty, Jacob Brodnik had a formidable temper. Fury blazed out of his deep-set eyes.

"You have wasted over an hour of my time, Mr. Honiwell, which is not important. But you have also been playing games with the mind of a man in acute distress," he glanced across at Gordon Cargill who, embarrassed, looked away, "—and with the life of a woman in desperate danger. This is not, I think, so easy to forgive. You owe it both to Mr. Cargill and myself to lay your cards on the table—*if* you have any cards to lay. Please tell us precisely how many men Scotland Yard *would* be prepared to give me."

Hating the position in which he found himself, Matt decided that he had no more room for maneuver.

"Mr. Brodnik, I have already explained that I am here purely as an observer. I have no authority to commit Scotland Yard to anything whatsoever."

Brodnik's eyes, perhaps the most expressive that Matt had ever seen, still registered fury, but mixed with it now was both disbelief and contempt.

"You are a man without authority? But you were introduced to me as *Chief Detective Superintendent* Honiwell. You must at least have *someone* under your command."

Matt was beginning to wish that he was anywhere on earth but here.

"I am not without authority, Mr. Brodnik. But I am also under authority. And my strict instructions, of which Mr. Cargill was well aware before I came, are that under no circumstances can I release even one man to follow up unsupported ESP information."

"Not one man?"

The fury died out of Brodnik's eyes. Everything died out of them. They became as blank as the glass eyes of a dummy, signaling, more plainly than anything else could have done, that the interview was over; Mr. Brodnik was through.

"In that case, Mr. Honiwell, it is a mystery why you bothered to come."

Of all things in life, Matt hated an icy withdrawal. Years of policy work in rough areas had taught him how to shield his sympathetic nature against all degrees of aggression. Against hard men, no one at the Yard could be harder. But withering disinterest or contempt seldom failed to get under his skin.

Flushing, he pushed back his chair and, hardly realizing what he was doing, started pacing Brodnik's consulting room. That in itself was an odd experience. The room was quite literally half-furnished. One end held three comfortable, if battered, easy chairs, a fire, a desk, and a standard lamp. But the light from the lamp, the room's only illumination, reached just about as far as the chairs and so did the warmth from the fire. At the point where the light and warmth petered out, so did the carpeting. Matt's pacing took him into this bare part of the room, and he found himself immediately in an uncannily different world. His footsteps rang hollowly on bare boards. The gloom rapidly became darkness. The temperature became not only cold, but dank: and suddenly he realized why. The windows at this end contained no glass and were boarded up. He touched one of the boards, and shivered. The wood was covered with a thin film of mold, and appeared to be crumbling with dry rot.

He glanced back, and saw that Brodnik was staring at him curiously. Good, thought Matt. Curiosity was better than coldness . . .

"You've asked me to lay my cards on the table, Mr. Brodnik," he said, his voice echoing eerily amidst all this bareness. "All right, I will. For the past hour I haven't just been hedging. I've been trying desperately—and failing—to get some information out of you about the *contents* of this ESP signal that you say you have received. If there is anything about that signal that corresponds with the facts of the case as we know them, particularly with some fact that you yourself couldn't have known, then I would have a powerful argument for getting my superior to reverse his decision. He'd do it, at the drop of a hat, if I could give him the slightest piece of tangible evidence to suggest that the signal was, so to speak, on the beam."

Slowly, wearily, Brodnik shook his head.

"I'm sorry, Mr. Honiwell, but ESP is not a 'positive proof' business. And no ESP man can function with a police organization that takes up an attitude of suspicion, skepticism, total disbelief. I think it would be better to terminate this consultation now. I shall not, of course, be charging any fee."

There was a terrible silence, but still more terrible was the expression on Gordon Cargill's face. He got up from his chair, and looked wildly, despairingly, from Brodnik to Honiwell, and then back to Brodnik. As he turned his head, his face was one moment in the light, the next in darkness, grimly symbolic of the hopes that had blazed up in him so short a while before and were now being brutally doused.

"For God's sake, Matt," he cried bitterly, "why did you make me go through with this thing? I was all ready to turn around and drive home when you—"

"What's that?" Brodnik asked suddenly. "Do I understand you to say that it was *Mr. Honiwell* who insisted you came in to see me?"

Gordon nodded. "He told me that I—I would never forgive myself if I didn't do everything possible to find Barbara. He almost forced me through your front door."

"Did he indeed?" Brodnik's expression had lightened. "That was distinctly odd behavior for a skeptical, hardheaded policeman. It seems that I may have misjudged you, Mr. Honiwell. You are more open-minded than I thought. You may even be, subconsciously, a believer. And when a policeman in a position of high authority is, consciously or subconsciously, a believer, there is always the possibility that he may convince others. This changes the situation entirely. I shall be most happy to tell you all that I know."

Gordon slumped back in his chair, his relief suddenly overwhelming. Matt, moving away from darkness to light, found himself breathing a silent prayer.

Once having decided, Brodnik was as good as his word, and described in detail the "signal," as he called it, that he had received.

"First of all, I must explain, very cursorily, the technique that I use. For a long period, often an hour or more, I concentrate my entire consciousness on the missing person. I consider this to be the psychic equivalent of sending out a radio transmission. Next, it is necessary to try and switch the apparatus, so to speak, from transmission to reception. I concentrate on nothing. I clear the mind absolutely, so that it is able to detect the slightest thought or feeling coming into it from outside.

"Now, always it is a *feeling* that I receive first; if adverse, it is a cold, dark feeling, which from long experience I recognize as a signal that my subject is dead. After that come the images: vivid, highly colored glimpses, bright as the brightest real-life scene, of how the subject died and where the corpse may be found. I might, for example, see a churning weir and the next moment a redbrick farmhouse. I call on the police. They give me a squad of men. We visit twenty, maybe thirty weirs. Finally we find one that is near a redbrick farmhouse. We drag the weir, we search the farmhouse and dig the grounds. Sooner or later the corpse comes to light. I am simplifying, of course, but, basically, that is my method. It has not often failed."

Matt nodded. He had done his homework and knew that Brodnik had a genuinely astonishing record of successes ... with corpses. There was no record that *he* had seen of his ever having led the police to a live victim.

Gordon leant forward.

"But this time the 'death' feeling didn't come?"

"No, Mr. Cargill. In its place, I had a definite sense of life ... a faint, flickering life fighting a desperate battle *against* death. It was so poignant, this feeling, that although I know little of your wife, I had no doubt that I was receiving the resonances, the echoes, of a brave woman's last struggle to survive. A struggle lasting not longer than twenty-four-hours."

"What made you give her twenty-four-hours?" asked Matt.

"That was a guess, no more."

"Based on what?"

Brodnik shrugged.

"The figure came into my head of its own accord. I cannot explain it. Discount it if you like. What cannot be discounted is the fact that this woman is nearing the limit of her ability—though not her will—to live."

For Gordon's sake, Matt abruptly changed his tack.

"There was something more?"

"Yes. There was . . . a vision."

"Just one?"

"Yes. And it was unlike any vision I have received before. Normally, as I told you, they are vivid—sharply etched and highly colored. This was vague and blurred. It swam in front of me almost as though I was in a delirium. But the outline was clear enough. I was staring at a country cottage, a romantic—how would you put it—'picture-book' country cottage. It had a flower-filled garden, a thatched roof, lattice windows— almost too much old-world charm to be true. It was situated halfway up a hill. Outside its front gate was what looked alike a main village street, and there was a signpost indicating that a place beginning with the letters SW was a mile and a half away. Further up the street, beyond the cottage, was a church with an oddly crooked steeple; or perhaps it was the waves of delirium that made it look crooked. I cannot be sure. Near it, the land sloped down to the sea. I glimpsed rocks, waves, wheeling seagulls. I could draw you a sketch of the place; in fact, I'll do so now." Brodnik turned to the desk, opened a drawer, and took out a sheet of paper. He drew a spidery impression of what he had described.

Matt's heart sank. It wasn't that Brodnik was a bad sketcher; but the result bore a painful resemblance to a chocolate-box artist's idea of an Olde English country scene. The hard-bitten, police-trained side of his mind told him that the whole thing looked as if it had emanated from a second-rate imagination. It just wasn't remotely likely that kidnappers would have kept a girl prisoner for six long weeks in such a setting. A barn, a disused farmhouse, a tumbledown shed or shack; *that* was the kind of hiding place they would have chosen, not a pretty-pretty cottage fronting on to a busy village street . . .

Brodnik himself seemed dissatisfied with the sketch. He shook his head over it and looked up at Matt a little ruefully.

"You feel there is something unreal about this? So do I. And I will tell you something even stranger: *nothing moved in this scene.* The waves of the sea, the wheeling seagulls in the air—they were motionless, frozen, all the time that I stared at them. It was almost as though I was looking at a photograph, and even I, versed as I am in ESP phenomena, can only wonder why. But this much I can tell you." Brodnik's manner became more positive, all the inner authority returning to his voice as he went on. "Beyond all doubt that vision, and that feeling of flickering, struggling life emanated from the same source. Find that cottage—and you will find Barbara Cargill. Reach it in time—and you will find her alive."

Suddenly he was staring at Matt and seemed to be peering straight into the Yard man's soul.

"You must believe me, Mr. Honiwell. And you must make this superior of yours believe. Otherwise, as I need hardly tell you, she will have no chance at all."

10

"No, Matt"

ALL THROUGH THE twenty-minute drive back to London, Matt Honiwell struggled to persuade Gordon that that last remark of Brodnik's had been a total exaggeration.

"Of course Barbara will have a chance, whether or not the Yard is able to help. For Heaven's sake, you and your father aren't exactly short of the ready, are you. You can employ inquiry agents by the dozen, and any competent private eye should be able to locate this spot Brodnik has described in no time at all." Matt was aware that he was talking with a forced heartiness; he was battling to conceal his own doubts, his feeling that even if this place was found, it was highly unlikely to turn out to be a kidnapper's hideout. To cover his confusion, he produced a notebook and started scribbling out addresses. "Look, here are the names of London's three top agents. The first two run a twenty-four-hour service. You can call them and start them working the moment you get back to your flat."

"But supposing the kidnappers take fright and move Barbara before we can track down this place? And even if we do track it down, if we don't have the police or the Yard's backing, who's going to break in and get Barbara out? Me—and a private army?"

"It might have to be that," Matt grunted, and was at a loss to think of anything else to say.

It was getting harder and harder to deny that *if* Brodnik's insight was true, the only thing that could save Barbara was a massive police operation: an operation conducted with speed and secrecy, aimed at locating that house and making a lightning raid before the kidnapping gang had the remotest idea that anyone was on their tail.

But no such operation could be mounted without Gideon's approval. And there was no getting away from the fact that Gideon simply wasn't going to give it.

Considering the improbability of Brodnik's "vision," or whatever he called it, Matt couldn't see how he could even *ask* Gideon to give it.

But suddenly he knew that he was going to try.

They had arrived outside the Cargills' London home. Since the kidnapping, Gordon had moved in with his father. The two of them shared a flat in a newly built luxury building in St. John's Wood. Gordon drove the Bentley into a multidoor private garage built exclusively for the residents of the building. Here Matt's own car—a battered Ford, as homely looking as Honiwell himself—stood waiting. It seemed absurdly out of place, cheek by jowl with some of the costliest cars in London.

Declining Gordon's invitation to join him and his father for a drink, Matt climbed out of the Bentley and walked toward his Ford. Gordon climbed out, too, and accompanied him across the garage.

"Thanks for coming along as adviser, and thanks for your advice," he said. "I only wish . . ."

"You only wish the Yard could help you more," Matt finished for him and nearly added, "So do I, mate. So do I."

He stopped himself, just in time. The policeman side of him remembered that the force must give a show of solidarity to outsiders. Instead, he said, "Here is the list of private investigators. Go ahead and ring them straight away. As for me—"

Hope flared up in Gordon's eyes.

"As for you? Does that mean the Yard might be taking action after all?"

"It only means that *I* shall be taking action," Matt said. "I'm going home to think things out, and then I'll ring Commander Gideon. Don't hope for too much. You'd be wise not to hope for anything. But what I can do, I will."

Gordon held out his hand.

"Thanks."

His voice was shaky with emotion, which wasn't surprising, Matt thought; few men could have been so torn with mental conflict as Gordon had been that night.

Feeling almost as desperately mixed-up himself, Matt climbed into the Ford and drove off swiftly. Half an hour later, he was home in the little Bayswater flat where he lived with Netta Honiwell, a woman who could not be his wife (her husband had long refused a divorce) but who had done the next best thing and taken his name. In his tricky domestic situation— especially awkward for a senior Yard man because of the risk of bad publicity or blackmail—no one had given him and Netta greater support and understanding than George Gideon.

Netta, a tall, striking-looking woman who had often put Gideon in mind of Kate, listened gravely while Matt poured out his problem. Then "Ring George," she said quietly. "Don't wait to think out what to say. Just ring him and let him know the whole position. He'll have the answer, if anyone does."

"He'll have it all right," Matt said sharply. Perhaps he was a little jealous of Netta's belief in the all-knowing George. "And I'm bloody certain what it will be."

Netta shrugged.

"Whatever it is, you'll feel better when you've confided in him. That's if you can reach him," she added suddenly. "He's involved in some business down on the Wellesley Estate. The last TV news showed a film of him making a speech about vigilantes." She smiled fleetingly. "He didn't only make a speech. In one shot, he was actually having a punch-up with some agitator."

Matt's misgivings deepened. He knew about the Wellesley situation, of course; the thought of that Estate—and the total breakdown of law and order there—was a shadow lurking at the back of almost every police-man's mind. If Gideon had been heavily involved in that, he'd be dead tired now, and this was the last moment to approach him. But if time was as short as Brodnik said—

Netta probably sensed his doubts. But if she did, womanlike, she airily dismissed them.

"While you're ringing George, I'll get you something to eat and a cup of tea. I bet you haven't eaten or drunk anything all day."

She walked into their bright little kitchenette, the door banging behind her as Matt started dialing Gideon's home number.

Penny came on the line. Her father and mother were both out, she reported. Kate was with a friend who had been taken to hospital, and George was at Wellesley police station, taking personal charge of an inquiry. In an emergency he could be reached there, she said, and she passed on the number.

Matt dialed it in a state of greater uncertainty than ever, but somehow he managed to infuse authority into his voice when a sergeant answered.

"This is Chief Detective Superintendent Honiwell. I would like to speak to Commander Gideon on a matter of extreme urgency."

"Just one moment, sir."

A moment was all it was before Gideon came on the line.

"Hullo, Matt. I had an idea you'd be ringing before the night was out. What did your seer see?"

It was entirely typical of Gideon that the moment Matt's name had been mentioned, everything else that had happened that evening dropped out of his mind, leaving him free to concentrate on the Cargill case alone. He sounded very tired, but that was the only sign that he had had a single other thing to worry about that night.

Encouraged, Matt embarked on a crisp, but detailed, description of all that Brodnik had said and the quandary in which he himself had been placed.

"The point is this, George," he ended breathlessly, "Since Barbara Cargill was kidnapped, we have several times pulled out all the stops— used literally thousands of men—following the faintest, feeblest leads. Now we've got a positive assertion from a man whose powers are highly respected by the police of three countries. I know it's unsupported ESP testimony—I have private doubts myself about its likelihood of being true—but surely to God we don't have to let Gordon carry the whole brunt of following it up?"

There was a pause. Then Gideon said slowly:

"What are you really asking me to do, Matt? Do you want me to authorize you to go to town on this, just as though it was a normal lead?"

"I suppose that's what it amounts to—yes."

Gideon's tone sharpened.

"You mean you want thousands of men—the two hundred Brednik asked for won't be enough—to drop all their other duties, however urgent, and start searching for a dream cottage halfway up a hill? And what do they do when they find it? What grounds would they have for applying for a search warrant? You haven't a shred of solid evidence to back all this up—and you yourself admit that the whole idea of kidnappers using a place like that as a base is beyond all feasibility! You'd be sending a vast body of policemen on an indefinite trip to Cloud-Cuckoo-Land. I can't take the responsibility for that. And I can't allow you to."

"But, George—"

"No buts," please, Matt. You've put Gordon Cargill on to the best private inquiry men in London. If they come up with anything *concrete*—the slightest hint, for example, that such a place really exists and that some questions really need asking about the behavior of its occupants—then I'll agree to the whole situation being reviewed. But until or unless that happens, there's only one answer I can give. No, Matt. *N-O.*"

The words came out in the famous Gideon roar, against which there was no appeal.

Gideon himself seemed to realize that he was treating Matt with unnecessary harshness.

In a somewhat modified tone, he growled, "When you've time to think it over, you'll see that I've only been talking common sense. You'll have to excuse me now. Got a lot on my plate at the moment."

There was a click as Gideon hung up, and the line went dead.

Matt stood, staring dully at the receiver. He had rarely felt more tired or more angry. He looked up and saw Netta standing beside him.

"So much for your all-seeing George," he snarled.

Not that it was in Matt Honiwell to be a snarler for long. A moment later, he was grunting "Sorry, love," as he gave her an affectionate peck on the cheek. A few moments after that, he was sitting opposite her in the kitchenette, enjoying ham and eggs. He was grateful for the meal. He needed food inside him before he faced the task of ringing Gordon and telling him that there was nothing whatsoever that the Yard was prepared to do.

GIDEON PUT DOWN the phone with a needling sense of guilt. He didn't

91

want to retract a word of what he'd said to Matt; but he needn't have been so abrupt. Neither was it strictly true that he had "a lot on his plate" here at Wellesley. He *had* had a lot, but the plate was almost empty now, with only the bare bones left—the final chores of what had been one of the most arduous evenings of his life.

The two civilian patrols had gone out on schedule, and two constables, under the watchful eye of Gideon himself, had been monitoring their walkie-talkie reports for more than an hour and a half. There had been no hint of trouble, and so far, at least, Riddell's alarmist forecasts had not developed.

Riddell himself had been packed off home in a police car, with instructions to get off to bed and to sleep the moment he got home. It had taken a fair amount of glowering and roaring on Gideon's part to get him to go; but Tom had suddenly found himself swaying on his feet and seen for himself the sense of Gideon's order.

With Riddell gone, Gideon had had to take personal charge of the night's routine investigations. He had gone down to the cells and spent some time questioning half a dozen trouble-makers from the meeting; boys who had been so violent and abusive that they had got themselves locked up for the night. Not that anything had come out of this questioning. He was up against that Wellesley stone wall that Riddell had so often complained about, and he found it every bit as impenetrable as Tom had done.

Other routine work had been proceeding in the Beresford's road. Under the supervision of Detective Inspector Dunne, two constables had gone from house to house in the hope of finding an eyewitness to the knifing of Eric Beresford, or at least to the dumping of his body on the pavement. But here, again, no information had been forthcoming.

A detective constable had also been sent to the house of Gerard Manley Hopkins. Gideon had been told that the gentle schoolmaster had rapidly recovered from his fainting fit in the interview room and had been driven home in a police car. It occurred to him that Hopkins would have recovered sufficiently to name those boys in Eric's form who had also had "See me" scrawled in their exercise books. The detective constable had been told to collect the list.

But it appeared that Hopkins had gone out somewhere, and his wife, Charlotte, had no idea where. Charlotte Hopkins seemed, in fact, distracted with worry about her husband; he was an inveterate pacer of streets at night, she said, and was simply asking for another attack. And suppose he fainted again?

The detective constable had done his best to cheer her up. He had told her that every spot on the Estate was now being passed either by a civilian patrol or an area car every nine to eleven minutes. He had then reported the incident by walkie-talkie direct to Gideon.

Gideon had listened with a groan. It seemed to him that he was getting nowhere. Then he remembered that ninety-nine percent of routine police work was like that. It was just that he wasn't usually as directly involved with it as he had been tonight.

The only hope of making real progress toward cracking the case seemed now to center around the hospital.

If Eric survived the operation, there was a chance that he might talk, and what he said could be extremely informative.

If John Rowlandes was accepted by the gang as a hero, and had callers at his bedside tomorrow, there was a chance that he, too, might learn a lot.

These were good prospects, but they depended on two very big "ifs."

Thinking of the hospital made Gideon remember Marjorie Beresford. And Kate.

Why hadn't Kate come through with some news before now? Surely the operation couldn't *still* be going on?

He lunged forward as the telephone rang, tensing as the constable on the switchboard announced, "It's Mrs. Gideon, sir."

Kate sounded strained, but her news was good.

Eric was out of the operating theater. The knife had been removed, and no irreparable damage appeared to have been done to the heart. But the boy had lost a lot of blood and was very weak.

"He's been given a sedative and is expected to sleep all night," Kate reported. "Marjorie won't hear of leaving him, so she, too, has been given a sedative, though a lighter one. That seems to leave me with nothing to do but come home."

"Glad to hear it," Gideon said heartily. "I'll come and pick you up myself. I think it's about time I called it a night. This has been, love, a distinctly busy evening."

"So I've heard," Kate said, just a trifle ominously. "Half the hospital has been talking about the way you punched that man in the audience. With all those television cameras focused on you, too."

The strain in her voice was now more noticeable than ever. Something was worrying her, and it was something about *him.* That was obvious. But what—

"George," she said suddenly. "The man you punched—his name's Fenton, isn't it?—was brought into the hospital hours ago. And . . . I'm afraid you may have done him more harm than you realized. He's—he's been detained for the night."

So that was all it was. The relief was so great that Gideon grinned.

"That was by special arrangement, dear," he said. "Thanks for worrying, but there's really no need to. I'll explain it all on the way home."

Explaining everything that had happened that evening took Gideon, in fact, from the time he met Kate until the time they were both in bed. Kate had seldom known him to give so long and detailed an account of his work; but then she realized that this hadn't been an ordinary evening. It had been a crisis, a major turning point in his career. He had met the vigilante challenge head-on, had created single-handed a new concept in civilian policing, and had begun to get to the root of the whole Wellesley Estate horror. And he had done all this against every kind of opposition, taking major risks and chances all the way.

Not often had Kate been quite so proud of her husband, but when she turned to tell him, heavy breathing told her that he was fast asleep.

For a man with so many responsibilities, Gideon usually went to sleep remarkably easily and, once gone, slept right through to seven A.M. Tonight, though, was an exception. Half an hour later he was suddenly wide awake again.

The sheets and blankets on his side of the bed were in total disarray, as though he had been tossing and turning in a frenzy.

He must have had a hell of a nightmare, Gideon thought, and nightmares were an extreme rarity with him; he could hardly remember the last one. Perhaps long years ago, after Kate had lost a child, and he had felt to blame—

He sat up in bed, trying not to wake Kate, and was astonished to find that his teeth were chattering.

He struggled to recall the dream, but for a moment, he couldn't.

94

Had it been about Marjorie Beresford? Or Eric? Or Tom Riddell? Or those civilian patrols, still circling the Estate in—if Riddell were to be believed—extreme danger? Or—

Baffled, confused, Gideon leant back against the headrest and closed his eyes.

And then it happened.

He did not only remember the dream; he half-dreamed it again.

He was in a high fever, some kind of delirium—so real that he actually began sweating again from every pore.

And through that fever, that delirium, he was staring at a beautiful country cottage, halfway up a hill.

11

Two O'clock

A MOMENT LATER, Gideon was fully and finally awake.

He remained perfectly still for five minutes, staring into the darkness and thinking deeply.

A more superstitious man would have assumed that he had had a direct ESP "vision." A less open-minded one would have put it down to the strain of the evening or Kate's lobster salad.

Gideon did neither. He simply concluded that his subconscious was greatly troubled, and it did not take him long to diagnose why. Because of the extreme pressure of events he had been guilty of what to him was a cardinal offense. He had given barely a thought to the mental anguish that Matt Honiwell and Gordon Cargill must be suffering.

Oh, he had an excuse. Insofar as he *had* thought about the Brodnik business, his chief concern had been to protect the CID from ridicule; to stop thousands of men wasting time on following bogus "psychic" leads. When Matt had tried to point out that Brodnik's leads had seldom proved bogus in the past, he, Gideon, had simply refused to listen.

But he had had no right to refuse to listen when he was dealing with the last desperate hope of a man like Gordon Cargill, a man who had trusted the police and gone on trusting them, all through the horror of a case that one newspaper had described as "the biggest Scotland Yard bungle of the decade."

His—Gideon's—subconscious had recognized this, and was paying him back by impressing on his mind what he had chosen to ignore.

He could not ignore that damned dream cottage now. His mind was so full of it that everywhere he looked in the darkness, he seemed to see its picturesque thatched roof; its lattice windows; the village street winding on, up the hill; the signpost showing that it was a mile and a half to SW—the church with a crooked steeple, the land sloping down to the sea.

His subconscious had built the picture, of course, from Matt's description. He wondered how it compared with Brodnik's pencil sketch. He would get the shock of his life if they were *exactly* the same . . .

Suddenly an idea occurred to him—an idea so simple that he must have been suffering from mental paralysis not to have thought of it before. There was one body of men in England who would be able to say almost at once if such a spot existed and describe its precise location, if it did. They were the police stationed in the seaside towns. It would be the easiest thing in the world to get the Yard's information room to radio these details to every seaside police station in the country. There would be no need to mention ESP, or the Cargill case, at all. A request for information about this place, to be sent as a matter of extreme urgency, was all that was necessary.

Gideon glanced at the dial of his luminous watch. It was five to two. If Brodnik's insight into Barbara Cargill's condition was correct, the poor girl only had a few hours to live. The message should be sent out instantly. There was always a chance that some sergeant or constable on night duty might know the place and come back with the answer straight away.

Still careful not to disturb Kate, Gideon slid out of bed and, pausing only to don his slippers, padded noiselessly downstairs, to the telephone in the hall. He was about to ring the Yard when he stopped, changed his mind, and dialed Matt Honiwell's number instead. Matt had better handle this job himself: only he knew the precise details of all that Brodnik had said.

The receiver at the other end was picked up instantly.

Netta Honiwell answered, and, when she heard who it was, her voice broke with relief.

"I kept *telling* Matt not to worry, George. I knew we'd be hearing from you before the night was out," she said.

Leaving Gideon wondering whether the whole world wasn't suddenly developing ESP.

"TWO O'CLOCK," THE millionaire Thomas Cargill said. A tough-looking, grizzle-haired man in his middle fifties, he stood, staring at his son with a mixture of acute concern and abject despair. "It is four hours since you left this man Brodnik. Four hours since Honiwell gave you a list of private detectives. And in all that time, you have not rung one of them. Not *one*. Why? Why?"

Gordon Cargill faced his father with the over-bright eyes of the hopelessly overwrought.

"I haven't rung them because they won't be any good," he said. "Scotland Yard is the one organization that can, and will, help us."

"But Honiwell telephoned and said—"

"I know, I know, father. But I didn't believe him." Gordon was shaking violently. It was obvious that he was barely in his right mind. "Can't you understand? *I just didn't believe him.* He's been with me all through this thing, every step of the way. He's not going to quit now. He's not going to let the *Yard* quit now, whatever obstacles this bastard Gideon puts up. I tell you, we've only got to hang on."

He slumped into an armchair in a near-total stupor. The ring of the telephone barely roused him, but at Matt Honiwell's words of victory his face showed the bewildered shock of a man reprieved.

"Gideon's given way," he whispered. "He—he's on our side. Barbara—Barbara's good as found, father—good as found."

"God help you—I only wish she were," Honiwell muttered, on the other end of the line.

Matt's own hand wasn't too steady as he replaced his receiver.

"Not so good," he said to Netta. "Gordon's blind drunk—and as far as I can make out, he hasn't contacted any private eye. Everything depends, then, on George's seaside coppers getting the sand out of their eyes. And," he added grimly, "on there being anything for them to see if they do . . ."

Still, he reminded himself, Gordon was right on one count. Gideon *had* come in on their side.

At that thought, Matt's hand became steady again. He dialed the Yard, and asked to be put through to Information.

"TWO O'CLOCK!" CHARLOTTE Hopkins greeted her husband. "What time do you call this to come home? Particularly after all you've been through.

God, darling, what are you trying to do to me? I've been *beside* myself with worry . . . Karen's not been able to sleep either. Worry in the house affects children, you know. She's been bawling nonstop since twelve."

Gerard Manley Hopkins smiled regretfully; but it was a distant smile, and when he spoke, he seemed to be delivering a sermon from a great moral height.

"I'm sorry to have caused you so much distress all around, but do try to understand, dear. I'm deeply concerned about this trouble on the Estate and must do my bit to stamp it out."

Charlotte—a quiet, intellectual-looking girl of thirty, normally rather prim and shy, but far beyond being either of these things now—became witheringly scornful.

"Do your bit to stamp it out? Heaven send me patience! Aren't you suffering from delusions of grandeur? Don't you remember that those vicious pupils of yours nearly stamped *you* out tonight? And by walking around and around the Estate, totally alone, totally unprotected, you're simply inviting them to make a proper job of it next time."

Gerard Hopkins's smile faded. He was deeply in love with his wife and hated upsetting her—not that he let that interfere with any purpose on which he had set his mind.

"I haven't just been walking around and around the Estate, my pet. I've been visiting one or two boys in their homes. Warning them that the police may be on their tails shortly. Interviewing them—trying to find out what *causes* this violent resentment against authority, against society . . . The only hope of curing them is understanding them, you know."

Charlotte took a deep breath.

"So you *recognized* some of the boys in that mob who attacked you. And instead of reporting them to the police, you've actually been calling on them individually, asking them what they meant by it. Is that right?"

Gerard nodded.

"That's more or less right, pet, yes. Of course, I've been talking to some of the parents too; that's what kept me so late. I explained that in my view, all this violence is much better dealt with by quiet, individual discussions, aimed at a fuller understanding of ourselves and the society we live in. If we adults have wronged these children, it is our obvious duty to ask them how and why. Ask for their forgiveness . . ."

"Forgiveness! Oh, God, Gerard, you, you make me want to scream. Don't you realize the risk you're running? There've been terrible things happening on this Estate tonight. One of your boys, Eric Beresford, has been knifed. He's in the hospital, fighting for his life."

Hopkins's dreamy, utopian gaze dropped violently to earth.

"Eric? Knifed? But who by? Who could possibly have a motive to—"

"Who could possibly have a motive to do *anything,* according to you!" Charlotte was on the point of tears. "Can't you *see* you're living in a dream world? That you can't, or won't, face reality? And—and if you go on pottering around the Estate, asking dangerous questions, and showing that you recognize dangerous people, then it's not going to be a razor next time. It's going to be a *knife!*"

But Gerard Manley Hopkins was not to be pried out of his cocoon of fantasy so easily.

"I would rather be a martyr to the cause of understanding than a betrayer of it," he said grandly. Then he walked past Charlotte into the kitchen and, somehow, lowered the tone of the proceedings by adding mildly, "Is it your turn or mine to make the Ovaltine tonight?"

Two o'clock.

Vittoria Orsini had no doubt that that was the time. It had been announced clearly enough by the striking clock on the mantelpiece of the bedroom. The clock was one of those elaborate, glass-cased affairs and the apple of her husband's eye. Vittoria wished that she could silence the wretched thing. It reminded her that every minute was ticking away Dino's life; and apart from that, it had tragic associations, because it had been a wedding present from Nicholas and Mario, her two brothers-in-law, now dead from the bullets of Jack Rocco.

How long would it be before Dino joined them? Not long, the clock seemed to say, its ticking suddenly sounding deafening across the silent room.

There was no other sound, except for Dino's breathing beside her—such heavy breathing. Thank God he had gone to sleep at last. Until now, he had been endlessly tossing and turning, and that hadn't been the worst of it. Every now and then he had started shivering, his huge body shaking the mattress down to its smallest spring.

Vittoria hadn't said anything; she didn't know what to say, what other arguments she could bring up to confound him, and so had simply pretended to be asleep.

"Maria, dear Mother of God," she prayed now. "I have a husband with the body of an elephant, the brain of a donkey, the courage of a mouse—and yet, with all that, the obstinacy of a mule. Guide and guard him tomorrow, I beseech you. Nicholas and Mario—perhaps, in the judgment of Heaven, they deserved to die. But Dino doesn't. He really doesn't. Holy Mother . . . save him . . . make him see sense."

"TWO O'CLOCK," THOUGHT the kidnapper of Barbara Cargill.

The hour had been tolled by a clock in a church tower that did not have a crooked steeple. The chimes had rolled out across Bognor Regis, a bustling holiday town that lies on a flat plain between the South Downs and the sea. The sound was faint by the time it penetrated the walls of Barbara's prison: the back bedroom of a secluded bungalow to the west of the town. The bungalow, an unpicturesque modern building, was far from any village street. The only road that came close to it was a private sand-and-pebble track leading down to the beach.

The kidnapper stood in the bedroom, staring down at Barbara, checking the church chimes with his watch and asking himself, for the thousandth time, how many hours of life the girl could possibly have left.

He had just given her a powerful injection of morphine, enough to keep her weak and helpless, and incapable of much in the way of thought or movement, for another twenty-four hours. He could easily have made it a lethal injection: one or two grains more would have done the job. But Leonard Lacey had begun his confused and dissolute career as a doctor and could not quite accept the thought of actually terminating a life.

It was crueler, of course, this way. The six weeks' hell of fevered helplessness that his injections had inflicted on Barbara could have been spared her, had he not lacked the nerve actually to kill.

But then, all through his life, failure of nerve had been Leonard Lacey's downfall. If he had not suddenly funked going out and collecting that ransom money, everything would have been different. He would be richer by thousands of pounds and would probably be living it up in South America. And if he had not shilly-shallied with Alec, Cliff, and Stewart, the other members of the kidnapping gang, they would not have run out on him the way they had; would not have left him, so to speak, holding the baby.

How long was it since they'd gone? Three weeks, four weeks, five? He had very little idea. Since then, he'd been almost as much a prisoner as his victim, going out only once a day for food and spending the rest of the time simply watching and waiting for Barbara to die.

It couldn't be long now. She hadn't eaten or drunk anything for twenty-four-hours. She hadn't spoken and had hardly moved. She didn't even seem to be frightened of his presence any more. Indeed, she hardly seemed to be aware of it.

She just lay staring at a picture hanging on the wall on the far side of her room. It was a sentimental scene, typical of a free-gift calendar, showing an old, thatched cottage with a flower-filled garden.

Savage, thwarted, undecided, Lacey clicked off the light and withdrew.

Barbara gave a faint moan of anguish as darkness blotted out the picture from her view.

12

Hunch

GIDEON AWOKE TO the sound of one newspaper after another being pushed through his front door letter-box and then thwacking down on the mat. That sound could only mean one thing: he had hit the headlines in a big way. Normally Gideon only took two morning papers—one, a paper of quality, the other a popular tabloid. But the newsagent, who was by way of being an old friend by now, always sent along with them a copy of any paper with a Gideon story on the front page. And it seemed as though this morning he had been accorded that dubious distinction by them all.

Donning slippers and dressing gown, Gideon stumbled downstairs. He had been right. There was a formidable pile of newsprint waiting for him.

He picked up three papers at random. "GIDEON'S HOME GUARD AGAINST CRIME" sprawled across one. "CID BACKS VIGILANTES —Bold Proposal by Gideon of the Yard," announced another. "YARD CHIEF IN VIOLENT PUNCH-UP," reported a third.

This third paper, a sex-and-sensation tabloid, seemed to be definitely against him. Under a lurid picture showing him apparently gloating over Rowlandes's unconscious body, it asked, "Is this the way to bring back law and order?" And it heavily stressed the fact that Rowlandes had been detained in hospital, adding in a slyly suggestive manner, "When asked how serious his condition was, the hospital spokesman said 'No comment' and cut off all communication."

Gideon winced and turned with a shrug to the other two papers. These seemed to be playing down the fisticuffs and applauding him for the originality and initiative behind the whole "Gideon's Force" concept. Slightly cheered, he walked into the kitchen, then filled and switched on an electric kettle. It was a rare thing for him to be up before Kate. Why shouldn't he make the occasion rarer by taking her up a cup of tea?

Long before the kettle boiled, he heard Kate coming down the stairs. This was followed by a pause. So, she was glancing through the papers. She came into the kitchen just at the moment when Gideon was filling the teapot, her eyes glowing.

"What a press you've had! Praise in paper after paper—and you deserve every word of it."

Gideon said drily, "One paper took a slightly different view."

"Oh, but that was because of the fight. When it comes out that that was a put-up job—"

"It'll be bouquets all the way? I doubt it, love. Fleet Street thrives on controversy, and it won't be long before it occurs to someone that Gideon's Force is the most controversial project in years. Think what they'd be saying if Tom Riddell had been right and there had been a sudden ambush, a bloody massacre, last night. I can't deny that, through me, civilian lives *were* put at risk. And they'll be put at risk again tonight. And every night, until this wretched Wellesley business is over."

Mention of this "wretched Wellesley business" put Kate immediately in mind of Marjorie Beresford and Eric. She wondered aloud whether seven A.M. was too early to ask the hospital for news.

"I hope nothing terrible's happened. I had awful nightmares about Marjorie last night."

"It was a night for nightmares," Gideon said and was on the point of telling her about his Brodnik dream and his two A.M. telephone call to Matt. But he stopped himself. There were limits to the number of his troubles that he could fairly unload on to Kate. Human problems haunted her far more intensely and persistently than they did him, and she had enough on her mind at the moment, what with this Marjorie affair—*and* the biggest wedding in Gideon family history getting nearer every day.

"I'll ring the hospital," he volunteered. "You go ahead getting breakfast."

106

He walked into the hall to telephone, leaving Kate to carry on the usual morning routine. When he returned to the kitchen, two minutes later, his face was grave.

"I'm afraid Eric's condition has 'deteriorated,' as they call it. There's been some unexpected complication, and he's lapsed into a coma. They may have to operate again today."

"Oh, my God! Poor Marjorie. If—if Eric dies, that woman's going to go clean out of her *mind.* I think I ought to go down there straight away."

"Steady," Gideon said. "There's no immediate danger, and the operation won't be until much later. I spoke to a staff nurse: they've got Marjorie in bed in a spare ward and are taking as much care of her as though she were a patient herself. If you went there now, you'd merely be in the way."

Hands deep in his dressing gown pockets, he stood, staring down at the preparations for breakfast, his mind far away.

With Eric in no position to name his attackers, the only hopes of a quick breakthrough in the Wellesley case now centered around John Rowlandes.

Or were there other leads that he ought to be following up? Supposing, for instance, he paid a call on that odd schoolmaster, Gerard Manley—

Gideon suddenly started.

What was he thinking about? *He* wouldn't be paying a call on anyone! His emergency takeover of the routine side of the Wellesley police investigations had ended. Riddell was back in charge today, and, if he knew Tom, he'd be around at the Estate already, checking up on the patrols.

Thoughts of Riddell occupied Gideon all through breakfast. Curiously enough, it was the second breakfast running that he had been haunted by the Riddell problem. Which meant that he had been dithering for more than twenty-four hours over whether or not to leave Tom on the case, and if there was one thing of which Gideon disapproved, it was dithering. He *had* to make a decision, once and for all.

But it still wasn't a simple decision.

On the one hand, it was undeniable that Tom had been a major hindrance to him last night. Not only had he become neurotically obsessive about the mysterious enemy on the Estate; he had seemed violently opposed to the whole concept of Gideon's Force. And, as chief detective superintendent on the case, he'd be required to organize that force night after night. Wasn't that an unanswerable argument for having him replaced?

On the other hand, over the last three months, Tom had poured more effort, energy, and determination into this case than ten other men put together. To take him off it now would deal his confidence a blow from which it might never recover. And as for his critical attitude last night—well, his grim predictions might have come true, might *still* come true. It would be a sad day when dedicated men were turned off cases just because they had the guts to speak their minds . . .

Gideon continued to agonize over the question all the way to Scotland Yard. But as soon as he got to his office, the issue resolved itself in the most satisfactory way possible.

Within a minute of his entering the room, the telephone rang, and it was Riddell on the line, ringing direct from the Wellesley substation. And before he had heard more than a few words, Gideon knew that he was talking to a very different Tom Riddell from the haunted, nervous wreck of the previous evening.

Perhaps it was having yesterday afternoon off, followed by an early night. Perhaps it was relief that nothing, after all, had come of his gloomy warnings. Perhaps it was a feeling that the end of the Wellesley case might at last be in sight. For whatever reason, Riddell was suddenly his old calm, confident self, with his brain—basically one of the shrewdest in the CID—functioning with greater clarity than ever.

He began by giving Gideon a crisp, incisive analysis of how he would like to improve the patrolling system the following evening. He suggested that the first patrols of the night should run from eight to twelve; that each patrol should carry at least two walkie-talkies; that they should be able to liaise by radio directly with the patrolling area cars, as well as with the police station; and that at least one member of each patrol should carry a truncheon. He had also worked out a slightly improved route for the patrols to take, which would mean less walking yet at the same time give more effective coverage of the Estate.

Hardly able to conceal his relief, Gideon gave these proposals his immediate approval. Then: "Oh, there's one other thing," Riddell said. "All through the early part of last night, until approximately two A.M., Gerard Hopkins was constantly spotted by the area cars, visiting various houses. He was noticed because he was the only private individual walking around on the entire Estate. I've checked up on the houses he was seen calling at, and I've compared the list with the Wellesley High School register that Harold Neame allowed me to see. Every house belongs to a parent of one of the boys at the school."

Gideon tensed. He had had an idea earlier that Gerard Hopkins' behavior might need looking into. Now he was sure of it.

"What do you reckon he's up to?"

"If you ask me, he's conducting a private, one-man inquiry into who attacked him last night."

"H'm," Gideon said. "You could be right. And a man like Hopkins wouldn't have the slightest desire to bring any of the culprits to justice. It's more than likely to be a kind of peace and love mission, an attempt at *understanding*." His tone sharpened. "But if he gets to understand too much, from the enemy's point of view, I doubt if *they'll* react in quite the same way."

"So do I," Riddell said. "I was thinking of having him tailed from now on, partly for his own protection, partly because we might learn something. Do you agree?"

"Wholeheartedly," Gideon said. "And—Tom."

The change in his tone indicated clearly that something personal was coming. He could almost hear Riddell tensing on the other end of the line.

"Yes?" he asked, nervously.

"I'd like you to know," Gideon said, slowly and deliberately, "that I think I'm very fortunate to have you on this case."

He replaced the receiver with Riddell's startled thanks still ringing in his ears and thought wryly what an overstatement that remark would have been, had he made it only ten minutes before.

THE RIDDELL PROBLEM off his mind at last, Gideon turned to the files that Alec Hobbs had placed on his desk—files of cases demanding his urgent attention.

There were only two of them. One was labeled "ORSINI" and the other "CARGILL."

The Orsini case. Ah, yes, *l'affaire Lemaitre,* he told himself, smiling at the memory of Lemaitre's volatile personality. He had promised him the previous morning—just twenty-four hours, though it seemed at least twenty-four weeks, ago—that he would contact Special Branch, to see if a way could be found of giving Dino Orsini total protection, while not interfering with his determination to be a human bait. Gideon had, in fact, telephoned the Special Branch commander half an hour after Lem had gone. But the commander, a smooth type called Ryan, was an expert in hedging, stalling, and diplomatic brush-offs. On this occasion, he had asked Gideon if he could ring him back and then had simply forgotten to do so. A furious Gideon had telephoned his office four times since, but on each occasion Commander Ryan had been out. All Gideon had been able to do was explain the situation, fully and patiently, to a superintendent, who appeared to be Ryan's assistant, and stress that a man's life very probably depended on the Special Branch coming up with something at least adequate.

The superintendent had not sounded impressed.

"The lives of presidents and prime ministers regularly depend on our decisions," he said blandly, and had promptly rung off, leaving Gideon in a state of impotent fuming.

It seemed, though, that his efforts had borne some fruit after all.

The "ORSINI" file contained a brief typewritten memo from Alec Hobbs.

Special Branch rang 5:25 P.M. They are sending their senior protection consultant, Major Davison, to see you tomorrow (Wednesday) morning at 11:30 A.M., if that is convenient. They add that he will have "positive proposals" to make re the Orsini situation.

"I should ruddy well hope so," growled Gideon to himself. But he was secretly pleased. To have stirred Special Branch into action on a criminal, rather than a political, case was no small diplomatic achievement, even for the CID's commander. Blood had been wrung from the stone. He hoped Lem would be duly appreciative.

A thought suddenly struck him, and, picking up the phone, he asked to be put through to Lemaitre, at the headquarters of the North London Division.

110

He explained about Major Davison's visit, and added, "It would save a lot of time if you could be there too."

"Well, well," said the irrepressible Lem, "a miracle at last. Suppose I bring Dino along with me? I'd like you to see him, anyway. Then you'll know just what I'm up against—two hundred and forty pounds of quivering, suicidal mania."

"With, from what you tell me, a streak of the rarest kind of courage," Gideon said. "Yes, Lem, I'd like to meet your Dino. See you both, then, at eleven-thirty sharp. Don't be late."

"What'll you do if I am? Call out Gideon's Force?" Lem asked innocently.

Gideon decided he had no answer to that and, grinning, slammed down the phone.

His grin faded as he turned to the file labeled "CARGILL." At the very sight of it his mood became confused and darkened. It contained a copy of Matt Honiwell's urgent request for information, circulated at two-fifteen A.M. to all seaside police stations, and clipped to this was a photocopy of Brodnik's sketch of his "vision": presumably Matt had had it delivered to the information room in the small hours, and it had been transmitted, along with the message, to all the seaside stations equipped to receive a radio picture.

Gideon stared hard at the sketch and tried to compare it with the cottage he had seen in his dream. He found it an impossible comparison to make; in memory, the details of his dream were too blurred. He had a feeling that there was some detail wrong—the church steeple bent in a different direction, the village street winding in a different way—but he couldn't be certain. Even the *attempt* to be certain gave him a feeling of unreality.

He turned with relief to the typewritten sheet that the file contained. This gave details of the response from the seaside stations so far—reports presumably sent by sergeants on night duty, glad of a chance to air their knowledge of their respective neighborhoods.

3:15 A.M. Ilfracombe. Cottage halfway up a hill at Combe Martin. Signpost near front door. But no church in vicinity, and it is passed by bridle path, not village street.

4:32 A.M. Morecambe. Seven cottages in neighborhood could be described as halfway up hills. All are in village streets. Signposts, churches lacking.

5:48 A.M. Sandown, Isle of Wight. Cottage at Bembridge might qualify. Close to sea, near a church, and halfway up a hill. But church has square tower and no steeple, straight or crooked . . .

There were seven messages in all, each starting off on a note of promise, then tailing off into lists of details lacking.

Were any of them worth investigating?

It suddenly struck Gideon that Matt was still under orders—his orders—*not* to investigate. The least he could do was modify those instructions in some degree.

He reached for the telephone and dialed Matt Honiwell's office. A tired, tense Matt answered. Honiwell had had scarcely a wink of sleep, because he had asked Information to telephone him immediately any report was received, and, as the typewritten sheet showed, reports had come in a steady stream all through the night.

"Brodnik hasn't slept much either," Matt said, not without a certain relish. "Every time a report came in, I telephoned him, to ask if he sensed that this was a genuine lead. So far, he's said 'no' every time. So I haven't seen any point in taking further action. Frankly, I'm just hanging on, hoping against hope that something more tangible may come in. And if and when it does . . ."

"You still want my permission to go to town?" Gideon hesitated for less than a second. "All right, Matt. You've got it. And don't think I've been converted by a vision, like St. Paul on the road to Damascus. My reasons are a lot simpler, and have nothing to do with ESP. I've decided that if I can't give a responsible, totally dedicated senior officer his head at a time of crisis, then I deserve to be put out to grass."

It was perhaps the closest to making a complete *volte face* that Gideon had ever come. Matt was so shaken that there was a long silence on the telephone. Then he started a fumbling attempt at thanks, which Gideon cut short with a gruff, "Never mind about that. Let's get back to the case. Have there been any more reports since this list was typed?"

"Just one." The sleepless night was telling on Matt. There was no mistaking the weariness in his voice, the flatness of complete despair. "It was so intangible, though, that I haven't bothered to ring Brodnik about it. Some young constable down at Bognor thinks—*thinks,* mind you—that he recently saw a painting by some local artist, depicting exactly the scene described. He can't remember where or when he saw this painting; he doesn't know the name of the artist, or even if he's alive or dead. The inspector in charge at Bognor has added: 'Inquiries are proceeding.' I'm half inclined to ring down there and tell them not to bother."

Gideon was about to say that he'd be inclined to do the same, when there was an interruption. The door of his office opened, and Alec Hobbs came in.

"Hang on a minute, Matt. What is it, Alec?"

"The Old Man's been on the telephone," Hobbs said, in an urgent whisper. "Wants to see you immediately. Sounds as if he's on the warpath."

Gideon started. Sir Reginald Scott-Marle and he had had a difficult relationship once, but recently a deep understanding had developed between them, the sort of understanding that made phrases like "on the warpath" seem childish rubbish. Yet Alec wouldn't have used the words without good reason. Scott-Marle's tone must have registered pretty unmistakable anger.

Gideon remembered the newspapers; how his face was splashed across all of them; how the whole country was discussing "Gideon's Force." He ought to have kept Scott-Marle in close touch with everything that had happened; should have telephoned an account to his home the previous night. He had been so busy he'd been guilty, to put it at its mildest, of grave discourtesy.

He stood up, startled and chagrined, and then remembered that Matt was still hanging on. Impatiently, he turned back to the telephone . . . and as he did so, his eye was caught by that Brodnik sketch, which was lying faceup on his desk. He was still staring at that sketch as he picked up the receiver, and suddenly he changed his mind about what he was about to say.

"Ring down to Bognor by all means, Matt," he found himself barking. "But don't tell them not to bother. Tell them to step up those investigations, to give them first priority."

"What?" Surprise swept all the weariness out of Matt's voice. "I don't get this, George. Why?"

"Call it a hunch," Gideon snapped. "Brodnik doesn't have a monopoly of them, you know."

Still not taking his eyes off the sketch, he put down the receiver.

"Call it a hunch," he had said, but it had been a policeman's hunch, founded on observation as much as intuition.

Although he had once played a part in saving a lot of the National Gallery's treasures, Gideon didn't claim to know much about art. But the longer he looked at that sketch—at the far too perfect pattern made by the cottage, the church, the general view—the surer he became that it was a glorified adaption of the picturesque rather than a real-life scene.

13

Human Bait

FIVE MINUTES LATER, Gideon was undergoing an experience that he had thought would never occur in his police career again. For the first time in more years than he could remember, he was—literally—on the carpet.

Scott-Marle was a tall, distinguished, man with a certain remoteness about him: only recently had Gideon begun to feel he knew him well enough to omit the formal approach he had hitherto accorded him. But now, accidentally or otherwise, Scott-Marle did not offer Gideon a seat but left him standing, for all the world like some defaulter on a charge.

"Commander," he began, with deceptive mildness. "I have called you in to refresh my memory on a rather important point. When we had a talk yesterday afternoon about the Wellesley case, I remember agreeing that, if the vigilantes meeting appeared to be getting out of hand, you should make a *tentative* proposal about a police-directed vigilante force. A *tentative proposal*, commander. A topic for discussion." The commissioner's manner sharpened. "I do not remember authorizing you to establish a new kind of special constabulary—still less, to enroll it, equip it, and send it out on immediate duty! I've had the Home Office on the telephone this morning, demanding an explanation. And I must warn you that the Attorney-General's office is of the opinion that setting up such a force, without government authority, is technically not within the power of the police to do."

Gideon's blood seemed to turn to ice. It sounded to him as though Scott-Marle was denying all responsibility for the concept; was failing to give him any sort of official backing.

He could hardly believe it, but whatever the situation, nothing would be gained by not holding his ground.

Returning the commissioner's steady gaze, he said quietly, "There can be no doubt that what that meeting was planning *was* illegal, before I stepped in." He went on to describe the anger of the walkers; the mood of bloodlust; the thinly veiled talk of lynching. "Do you seriously suggest, sir, I could have changed all that by merely offering them a topic for discussion? There had to be a positive program of action, one that could be put into immediate effect. That was what I gave them; that was what I understood that you had agreed that I could give them. And having given it, I was morally obliged to carry it out. I'm sorry that, in the heat of events, I omitted to make a special report to you, but for all else I see no reason for apology. Last night, from the time patrolling started, onward, was the first quiet night the Estate has had since Uniform gave it saturation policing. In effect, all I have done is return to the 'saturation policing' policy—with the difference that the people of the Estate now do some of the policing themselves. At their own urgent insistence. If that's against the law—"

"Then the law is an ass, eh?" For the first time, there was a hint of understanding in Scott-Marle's manner. "Thank you, commander. You've certainly given me a line on what to say to the Attorney-General's office. But there is another matter they might raise that I might find it a little harder to clarify."

The commissioner opened a drawer in his desk and produced a copy of the tabloid paper with Gideon's K.O. blow splashed all over the front page.

"Do you call *that* a contribution to a quiet night?"

A little less sure of himself, Gideon launched into a full account of the Rowlandes incident. At the end of it, a seeming miracle occurred. The commissioner appeared to be on the point of smiling.

"Sit down, George," he said. (It was always a good sign when "commander" turned to "George.") "Between ourselves, I don't mind confessing that in your shoes, I would probably have obliged young Rowlandes with a punch on the jaw myself." His face became grave. "But there's one thing you did last night that I could never have done."

116

Gideon glanced up sharply, prepared for the worst. It was one of the biggest surprises of his life when Scott-Marle stood up, came around the desk, and extended his hand. As Gideon took it, he said handsomely:

"No one but you could have turned an ugly mob scene into the start of a completely new chapter in police history. You used the highest skill, and it was unpardonable of me to mistake it for high-handedness."

"It was unpardonable of me," Gideon responded, "not to have kept you more closely in the picture."

Scott-Marle, turning back to his desk, gave the ghost of a grin, "There I must agree with you. I do not feel completely in the picture yet. And won't, until you have provided me with a full report, detailing the need for this special emergency force, its duties, its limitations, its complete modus operandi. And I'm afraid it must be good enough to stand the closest examination, not only by our own legal department, but the Attorney-General and the Home Office experts, too. Do you want to be relieved of all your other duties for, say, twenty-four hours while you get on with it?"

Gideon thought of Lemaitre and Orsini, due in his office almost immediately. He remembered Matt Honiwell and Gordon Cargill, following incomprehensible leads, with time running out on their last desperate hopes. He had a composite mental image of the people in the Wellesley case: the now-confident but still vulnerable Riddell, John Rowlandes, Marjorie Beresford, Gerard Manley Hopkins, and the Gideon's Force volunteers themselves. It looked as though the mysterious enemy on the Estate had been checked—but for how long? It was possible, even probable, that it would strike back; and that blow was more than likely to come tonight.

"I know no one's indispensable," he said at last, "but I honestly doubt if I can be spared for the next twenty-four hours."

The faintest of smiles relieved the curtness of Scott-Marle's tone.

"Curiously enough, George, I honestly doubt it too. So I'm afraid you'll have to tackle the report on top of everything else. That's the sort of penalty one pays for making history . . ."

Gideon left with his right palm still tingling from the warmth of that Scott-Marle handshake. And his spine still tingling from the ice that had so recently—if so completely—melted away.

When he got back to his own office, he found that Scott-Marle had

117

already taken action to help him. He had sent around Sabrina Sale, the most efficient secretary in the building—a woman whose services were so highly prized that they were shared by all the senior men in the CID, each of them calling her in when there was some high-pressure paperwork to be done at high speed. Gideon was never entirely sure that it was only Sabrina's professional services that were shared. He was never entirely sure of anything with Sabrina; not even whether he ought to feel quite as he did about her.

She was a beautiful woman, probably just into her fifties, with a flawless figure and a gentle, mischievous air that belied her formidable reputation for efficiency.

Everything she said disturbed Gideon; and sometimes he suspected it was aimed to do just that.

"Commander," she told him now, "I've been ordered by the commissioner to put myself entirely at your disposal, for as long as you want—er, require me."

Sabrina's switch from the all-embracing "want" to the businesslike "require" was accompanied by a smile that somehow succeeded in being both demure and a covert invitation. Or was it only his imagination that made it seem so?

Gideon took a deep breath and told himself severely that he really had enough on at the moment without this kind of complication.

"Thank you very much, Sabrina. I may well be wanting—er, requiring you very shortly. May I ring for you when I do?"

"Of course, commander. I'll be standing by from now on."

When Sabrina had gone, Gideon walked to his desk, by no means unimpressed, and picked up the telephone. He rang down to the canteen and asked them to send up coffee and biscuits for four. The Lemaitre-Orsini-Major Davison meeting was likely to be a tense session; coffee and biscuits would help to establish a calmer atmosphere. He glanced at his watch and saw that it was just before eleven-thirty.

Lemaitre and Orsini, who had had to travel halfway across London, arrived dead on time; Major Davison, who had only to stroll from another part of the Yard building, had not shown up after ten minutes. Another example, thought Gideon, of the Special Branch trying to put the CID in its place, and he took a childish pleasure in seeing the major's coffee cooling in its cup.

In a way, though, he was glad to have the opportunity of a few minutes alone with Lemaitre and Orsini. He needed to confirm for himself that the extraordinary things he had been told about the Italian were true.

At first, it seemed hardly possible that they could be.

Dino came blundering into the room, looking for all the world like a not-very-funny stage comedian. He was so nervous that sweat was already beading his forehead as he said, "Good morning, commander. Is great pleasure meeting you." As he advanced to shake Gideon's hand, he knocked against a chair.

Gideon helped him to straighten it and noticed in the process that the man's whole body was shaking. He looked away with a mental shrug. The very idea that this crazy character would be capable of actually going through with anything dangerous was surely preposterous.

"Mr. Orsini," he said crisply, "Mr. Lemaitre has told me about your courageous offer to turn yourself into human bait. But there are some things I must point out to you. This is not Sicily, nor is it old-time Chicago. The CID is perfectly capable of taking care of men like Jack Rocco on its own. We have had our eye on Rocco for a long time, as a matter of fact, and we are only waiting for him to make one slipup—"

Dino suddenly spread his arms wide.

"Slipup? Why wait for a slipup? I give him a bloody big *push!*"

Out of the corner of his eye, Gideon saw Lem bury his face in his hands in a comical gesture of despair. He decided that it was high time to cut out this element of farce. Too much stark tragedy lay underneath and was showing through.

"Are you sure you won't be making a bloody big fool of yourself, Orsini?" he said sharply. "If you arrive at this Jack Rocco's pub and start shaking and falling about as you've been doing here, all you'll get for your pains is a punch in the stomach or a clout over the head, and the intense strain and anxiety you've caused your wife and family—to say nothing of the trouble you're causing Mr. Lemaitre—will have been in vain."

Orsini sat down heavily on the nearest chair. His shivering did not stop—on the contrary, it started the whole chair quivering—but a subtle change had taken place. Gideon had the distinct impression that he was shaking not from fear, but from an inner passion that came close to fury.

"It is not true that Jock Rocco's mob will laugh at me. And I tell you why. I have worked out a story that will put the bloody wind up them. I shall say that my brother Mario left me enough incriminating evidence to put Jack and all his top men inside for good. I shall say that unless Rocco pays me a big sum of money—ten, fifteen, twenty thousand pounds—in twenty-four hours, that evidence goes to the police." Suddenly Orsini's voice became remarkably steady, and his eyes had a positively dangerous glint. "It is true that when I say all this, my voice will croak and my body will be doing the shakes. But what harm will that do? I am delivering an ultimatum to the murderer of my brothers. It is natural that I show *some* fear. All that matters is that my message is delivered to Rocco loud and clear. And I tell you exactly what he will say to himself when he get it. 'These Orsinis are nothing but trouble. But I have killed two of them, and got away with it. Why should I not do the same with the third?' And he will order his hatchetmen out without thinking twice about it. Do you not agree that this will be so?"

Gideon frowned and glanced at Lemaitre.

"What do you think, Lem? You've had dealings with Rocco."

Lemaitre didn't hesitate.

"This will be so, all right, with a ruddy vengeance! If Dino gets near any of Rocco's henchmen and delivers that spiel, there's no one in Soho who'd give twopence for his chances of living through the next twenty-four hours."

"That I don't mind," Dino said simply, "as long as I am the last person whom Rocco ever kills."

Gideon could not help being impressed, but he did his best to dissuade the plump restaurateur.

"You can't tell me your wife shares those feelings. Have you asked yourself if you are being fair to her?"

"Repeatedly, Commander, but you see—Nicholas and Mario had wives and children too."

There was a tense pause. Gideon, defeated, retreated behind his biscuits and coffee. The biscuits stuck in his throat; he gulped down the rest of the coffee and then turned to Lemaitre.

120

"What measures have you in hand at the moment to protect Mr. Orsini?"

Lemaitre produced a typewritten report from an inside pocket and put it on Gideon's desk.

"They are all spelled out in detail there. Basically, I've done three things. Mr. Orsini's car, a dark green Volvo, has been down at a garage in Islington all night, being discreetly bulletproofed by a couple of boys I know who are expert at that sort of job."

Gideon raised an eyebrow but made no comment. He was fairly sure that the "boys" referred to were normally employed for less respectable purposes; probably the garage was a place where stolen cars were worked on all night, and given face-lifts that made them unrecognizable. But Lem worked in a tough area and often had to get results by unorthodox means. The results were what mattered.

"What else?" he asked.

"I've got the Finchley CID on the move. They've taken over the first floor of an empty shop opposite Orsini's restaurant and are all set to turn it into a stakeout. If Rocco attempts any sort of a raid there, he'll get quite a surprise. Also, the Finchley inspector is going to have six men on standby for the next twenty-four hours, ready to follow Dino on foot or by car. It's there, of course, that the problems start."

"What problems?" Dino asked innocently.

"Let me spell them out for you, Mr. Orsini," Gideon snapped. "A bodyguard, to be effective, would have to remain within five feet of you at all times. But to be unnoticed, he'd have to follow twenty or even thirty feet behind you—and what use would he be then? Or suppose you were in a car. Even a bulletproof car can be ambushed or rammed. For real protection, a police car ought to keep right on your tail. But for the Rocco men not to spot it, it would have to be all of fifty yards behind. I've got to confess that I simply don't see—"

He broke off as the door opened and a tall, military-looking man strode into the room. He was wearing a raincoat that had seen better days and carrying the regulation black case that no businessman, from executive to tax collector, is ever seen without.

There was no room for doubt that this was Major Davison, thought Gideon. Only a member of Commander Ryan's staff could behave with such high-handed arrogance. It was evident that he had been standing outside the door, eavesdropping, for some time before he had come in.

"An interesting summary, commander," he told Gideon, "but at least two years out of date. With a new technique the Israelis have developed, the bodyguard can be anything up to *a hundred yards* away."

14

Iron Raincoat

THERE WAS A sudden, startled silence, broken finally by Lemaitre.

"Then what the hell does he do when someone attacks the body he's guarding? Pole-vault?" he asked.

Major Davison laughed, with the casual indulgence of a film star.

There was, in fact, a lot about this Davison that reminded Gideon of a film actor of the David Niven/Douglas Fairbanks, Jr. era. He had the handsome, bronzed face, the trim mustache, the nonchalant air of elegance. Gideon guessed that his age was somewhere between the late fifties or early sixties and that he'd gone to Special Branch after retirement from Military Intelligence. The romantic spy in person, he thought sourly. In other words, an overgrown glamour boy, who went through life imagining he was taking part in a James Bond film.

"We'll probably have to find a new name for 'bodyguard,'" Davison was saying. "This new technique eliminates a lot of the need for physical guarding. Let me show you."

He whipped out a flick knife and proferred it handle first.

"Take this and try to stab me through the chest."

Gideon complied to the request with speed and vehemence. On touching the major's raincoat, the knife simply glanced off, falling harmlessly from Gideon's hand.

Davison smiled sardonically, as if he'd guessed Gideon's summing up and was amused.

"This coat is made of a new material, a spin-off from the American space program. They've found a way of reinforcing polystyrene with steel filaments, on something of the same principle that's used for reinforcing concrete. The result is a lightweight garment that can protect against razors, knives, bullets, anything up to, and including, a burst from a Sten. An 'iron raincoat,' the Israelis call it. Try it on, Mr. Orsini. I gathered you were a big man, so brought one that I thought would be your size."

As the major slipped off the raincoat, Orsini jumped up and once again his chair went flying. This time, however, it was the clumsiness of enthusiasm, not nerves. It was obvious to Gideon that the plump, would-be victim had been secretly despairing of his life. Now that hope of survival was beginning to dawn, he was a changed personality. He handled the "iron raincoat" as reverently as though it was an instrument of salvation straight from Heaven: his mouth opened and closed as though he were sending up silent prayers of thanksgiving.

"Feel the lining," the major said. "It's got an inch of padding over the chest and stomach. It doesn't give a hundred percent cushioning against bullets—nothing could. You might end up with a cracked rib, or body bruises. But one thing I can guarantee. Whatever the caliber of the bullet or the velocity of the gun, there'll be no penetration."

"Unless," Lemaitre said grimly, "they aim for the head."

The major was not in the least put out.

"They seldom do, you know. Except in the case of highly trained political assassins, gunmen instinctively go for the body first. Their later shots—say, the third, fourth, and fifth—may be aimed higher. But by that time the subject will have dropped flat on the ground (which we recommend) or there will be what the textbook calls 'distracting action' by the bodyguard."

"From a hundred yards away?" Lem said derisively. "He'll be lucky if he even hears the shots!"

"He'll hear them all right," Davison said, with nonchalant confidence. "He's only *physically* at a distance from his subject. Electronically, he's never more than a whisper away." He turned down the right lapel of the raincoat and pointed to a slight bulge in the lining. "There's a microphone-transmitter built in here. It has a range of between a hundred and a hundred and fifty yards, and the signal it gives is so powerful that a bodyguard can home in on it through the walls of a building, or even if he's in a following car."

"Now just a minute," Gideon said. "Let's suppose the bodyguard is on foot, tailing the subject through the streets. We know he's got to remain inconspicuous, but how can he? Surely, if he's listening to some walkie-talkie contraption as he goes along, he'll be the most conspicuous tail in history."

The major shrugged. Hey Dude, What's the deal, MAN!
"Don't fret, commander. We have the answer to that, too."

He picked up the slim executive case that he had been carrying on his arrival.

"All the bodyguard has to do is carry this. Not a very noticeable item, I think even you would agree. You'll see thousands of businessmen with cases just like it at every commuter train station, in every rush hour. Inside, though, it's just a little—unusual."

He snapped the case open, revealing a mass of electronic equipment.

"Essentially, this is a high-powered shortwave receiver, with built-in tape recording facilities. It can pick up the faintest signal from the bug in the subject's lapel, magnify it, and retransmit it to a miniature receiver, no bigger than a pea, that fits right inside the bodyguard's ear. The miniature receiver is finely adjusted so that no sound escapes *from* the ear. So if the bodyguard happens to be in close proximity to other people—in a crowded bus, say, or a jam-packed pub—he can still switch on and listen in to his subject, without anyone around suspecting what he is doing. Ingenious, don't you think?"

"That's just about the word," Lemaitre said softly. The superintendent's normal expression—alert, cocky, skeptical—had subtly altered; it had begun to register a touch of schoolboy awe. There was a side of Lem that had never really grown up—that seldom, in any man, grows up—and to this side, all this gimmickry was having an irresistible appeal.

Gideon himself was hardly less deeply impressed. He found his exasperation with Davison ebbing away, replaced by an awareness that he was in the presence of a supreme professional. Offhand they might be—but Ryan's men knew their stuff.

"You mentioned tape-recording, major."

"Ah, we're coming to that. Supposing someone steps up to the subject and says something threatening or suspicious. The distant bodyguard will not merely hear it—by pressing a catch by the handle of the case, he can tape it on the spot. In fact, he can tape everything that happens to the subject, if he chooses."

"Just like a recording angel, eh, major?" Dino said. He was the new, transformed Dino, grinning, laughing, bouncy as a balloon in a skittish wind. "With a bodyguard like that behind me and this 'iron raincoat' around me, I'll feel as safe as houses, safe as a hundred houses! Must I wait for tonight to deliver my ultimatum? It is past twelve. The Rocco place will be open. Why shouldn't I get it over and done with *now*?"

"I'll tell you why," Gideon said sharply. "We haven't had a chance to select, let alone train, a—er—recording angel to follow you."

In this new, excited mood, Dino brooked no discouragement.

"Couldn't Mr. Lemaitre do it, just for now?"

Gideon struggled to control his outrage. Mr. Lemaitre, he was going to point out, was a chief detective superintendent who had left guarding and shadowing jobs behind him thirty years ago. But before he could even form the sentence in his mind, Lemaitre had taken the executive case from the major and was being shown how to fit the miniature receiver in his ear.

"It'll be like old times, doing a bit of tailing," he remarked wistfully.

Like old times . . .

The years fell away, and Gideon suddenly saw Lem as a young fellow sergeant, bursting to try any and every new approach, but always being trapped by that fatal impulsiveness, always ending up with an unfair black mark against his name. Equipment might have become electronic, radio receivers miniaturized, raincoats given a space-age bulletproofing, but the Lemaitres of this world remained eternally unchanged.

Gideon was not going to discourage him again. He turned to Dino.

"Well, if you *must* go through with this lunatic business, good luck to you."

For Lemaitre, he had only a half-rueful grin, but its message was exactly the same.

AN HOUR LATER, Lematire was taking the strangest stroll of his life.

126

He was wandering around Soho in the gray light of a lunchtime drizzle—a light to which the neon signs above a dozen strip clubs were imparting a blowsily erotic tinge.

Outwardly the stroll was perfectly normal. One moment he was pausing to inspect the window of a luxury sex aid boutique. The next, he was asking the owner of a Hungarian restaurant what business was like these days.

Yet he had not noticed a single item in the boutique window. He had not heard a word of the Hungarian restaurant owner's answers to his questions.

All the time, his head had been filled with a stream of voluble Italian: the sound of Dino Orsini delivering his ultimatum at the bar of a public house called Punchinello's, about a hundred yards away around the corner to his left.

Punchinello's. Lemaitre smiled wryly at the aptness of the name. Dino was committing his act of mad bravado in a place called after the world's most tragic clown . . .

Not that Dino's performance sounded tragic. Lemaitre knew little or no Italian, so could not understand what was said, but the words were pouring out with the force—and ferocity—of bullets. So much so, that suddenly they seemed to be splitting his eardrums.

Glancing up, Lemaitre realized what had happened. Almost subconsciously, he had started strolling toward Punchinello's. He had already rounded the corner, and the pub's entrance—a slitlike doorway sandwiched between a Greek delicatessen and a cinema showing decidedly indelicate continental films—was now directly ahead, about fifty paces farther along the pavement. This meant, of course, that the executive-case receiver he was carrying was getting uncomfortably near the source of its signal. He turned it down. At the same time, he slowed his pace. Shouldn't he go by the major's rules and keep a hundred, or at any rate, fifty yards away?

Or didn't rule books apply when one's subject was deep in enemy territory and deliberately goading that enemy into planning an attempt on his life?

It was an uneasy thought; and an uneasier one followed it.

Why were Rocco's men allowing Dino to go on so long? He had been speaking, almost without interruption, for nearly twenty minutes. And whatever he was saying, it wasn't likely to make enjoyable listening for a

Rocco henchman. Perhaps they were egging him on, deliberately keeping him talking, while one of them slipped out and contacted—

At that moment, Dino's stream of Italian was interrupted by a soft, smooth voice, speaking English with a slight American accent.

"Mr. Orsini? I am Ron Curtis, manager of Punchinello's. I understand you had a message awhile back for Mr. Rocco."

Lemaitre abruptly remembered his role as "recording angel." He pressed the catch by the handle of the executive case that started the built-in cassette recorder and was just in time to tape one of the most chilling invitations he had ever heard.

Still in the same soft voice, Ron Curtis was saying: "Well, your message has been delivered, Mr. Orsini. And if you'll be kind enough to step upstairs, Mr. Rocco is waiting to give you his reply—in person."

15

Between the Eyes

THERE WAS SILENCE, followed—to Lemaitre's horror—by the sound of a door opening and at least two persons' footsteps going upstairs. So the fool was walking straight into the deathtrap. Why? He hadn't had to. He'd been in a public bar. He'd been wearing a raincoat that, on Major Davison's assurance, was a seventh wonder of the universe. It should have protected him long enough for a quick dash to the street . . .

Most likely, Orsini was once again being fuddled by his own peculiar streak of obstinacy. The prospect of meeting Rocco face to face and openly accusing him of his brothers' murders . . . with the knowledge that every word was being taped by Scotland Yard . . . must have seemed an opportunity more important than life itself.

In an obscure way, Lem still felt a kind of admiration for the man, but that didn't alter the fact that Orsini had landed him with one of the trickiest problems of his career.

He needed to contact a police station, or better still, an area car, fast. But he had no walkie-talkie on him. His car, which was equipped with a police radio, was parked near Soho Square, two hundred yards behind him. A dash toward it would take him clean out of range of Orsini's microphone . . . and God knew what might have happened by the time he was back in contact.

Orsini had climbed the stairs now. The man who was with him, presumably the soft-voiced Ron Curtis, tapped on a door.

A new voice—high-pitched for a man, yet too harsh and grating for a woman—called out: "Ah, Mr. Orsini, come in."

Lemaitre remembered that Jack Rocco talked like that. It had given rise to rumors that he was some kind of sexual pervert, but no one knew for sure. The next remarks left no doubt about the speaker's identity.

"I don't believe I've had the privilege of meeting you before. But I remember both your brothers very well indeed . . ." The voice became both higher-pitched and harsher. "They made a great impression on me. And, as I think you know, I finished up by having quite an impact on *them.*"

The following moment was one of the eeriest Lemaitre had ever known. He heard a heart thumping and a heavy, strangled attempt at breathing; and both sounds seemed as close, as intimate, as though the heart and the lungs to which he was listening were his own. But they weren't, of course. The highly sensitive lapel microphone was simply picking up the sounds of Orsini himself, in the grip of a near-pathological fury.

What happened next was almost foreseeable.

A roar of anger from Dino's throat erupted in Lemaitre's eardrum. There were more heavy footsteps, obviously caused by Dino rushing forward, making, from the sound of it, a bull-like charge straight at Rocco. There were other footsteps: Rocco's men, presumably, hustling to intervene. There were blows, shouts, screams—but Lem suddenly wasn't listening to them; he was making a bull-like charge of his own along the pavement.

Less than five seconds later, he was inside Punchinello's main bar. This was a long, narrow room with a poorly lit bar running down the whole length of one side. The rest of the room was almost totally unlit, apart from three or four candles in the necks of Chianti bottles, adorning the tops of the upended wine barrels that served as tables.

Four or five men were standing at the bar, being attended to by a pert Italian girl. At one of the wine-barrel tables, a youth and his girl were kissing in a pool of darkness that they had created by blowing out their candle. Otherwise, the place was empty.

Lemaitre went straight up to the bar. The sounds of the fight going on upstairs were still, literally, ringing in his ears. It sounded as if Dino— helped, no doubt, by the raincoat—was holding his own; but his stentorian

130

breathing showed that there was no way in which that situation could last for long.

The men at the bar glanced up. None of them spoke, but Lem hadn't much doubt that they recognized him. He certainly knew two of *them*: Spike Graham and Jack Riley, two of the toughest hoods around Soho.

"Right, boys, I'm going upstairs," Lem stated flatly. "If no one tries to stop me, no one gets booked. Simple as that. Okay?"

There was a door to the right of the counter. It stood ajar. Lem thought he could glimpse stairs leading up beyond. He started to walk toward it.

Spike Graham and Jack Riley, and one of the other men, heaved themselves off the bar counter and blocked his way, the pert Italian girl, with eager cries, egging them on.

Upstairs, Jack Rocco was shouting: "That's right, get his arms. Twist them, break them if you can!"

Lemaitre heard both shouts at equal strength, one through his left ear and the other through his right. He began to feel dizzy and remembered that the ears controlled one's gyroscopic balance. People weren't built to be in two places at once . . .

Then three things happened that were enough to clear anyone's mind.

Spike Graham produced a revolver. Jack Riley picked up a beer bottle, casually smashed it against the counter, and held the jagged remnant within a foot of Lemaitre's face. The third man was fingering a knife.

Lem was not unarmed. He had drawn a regulation 9-mm Walther automatic from the Yard storeroom before setting out for Soho. But he doubted if he would get a chance to get at it.

He had, in fact, only one thing to rely on: his agile Cockney wit. It did not fail him.

"Smile, lads," he said breezily. "You're on 'Candid Camera.'"

And he opened the executive case, to show them the mass of electric wiring, the turning spools.

"Believe it or not, this gadget is relaying your faces and your voices direct to West End Central police station. They'll be radioing an area car now. You've got less than a minute before it gets here—and no chance of avoiding a five-year stretch if you so much as lift a finger—"

He broke off, letting a soft electronic whirring from the heart of the apparatus build up the plausibility of his story.

Startled panic crossed their faces. Even before he snapped the case shut, they had moved back out of his way, and a split second later he was rushing the stairs.

There was one person he had forgotten, though: the girl behind the counter. Out of the corner of his eye he saw her press something. An alarm bell started shrilling in the room upstairs, somewhere close to the microphone; it sounded as though it was exploding in the center of his head.

Transferring the executive case to his left hand and holding the Walther in his right, Lem was halfway up the flight when he heard Jack Rocco issuing emergency instructions to his men. The last of these orders momentarily stopped him dead.

"Orsini mustn't be able to say a *syllable* to the police when they find him. There's only one way to be sure of that. Aim at the forehead, or better still, between the eyes . . ."

Lem pulled himself together; took the remaining stairs two at a time.

But he wasn't fast enough, not by half.

Two shots rang out before he reached the top, and his right eardrum resounded to an earthshaking thud—the fall of Orsini's massive body, magnified by the effect of the microphone falling with him to the floor.

SO MUCH FOR the iron raincoat.

So much for the whole concept of a "recording angel" bodyguard, functioning at a distance.

So much for the oh-so-elegant Major Davison and all his poufy theories.

And so much for him, Lemaitre, for behaving like an impressionable adolescent and believing them . . .

Lemaitre arrived at the top of the stairs feeling physically sick with a sense of failure and self-disgust. There was a strong smell of cordite everywhere. He could actually see blue gunsmoke coming from under a door directly across the landing.

Not much doubt, then, where Rocco and his hatchet men were.

Lem crossed to the door and, putting the executive case down on the floor (it was useless now—the microphone seemed to have gone dead, with its wearer), tried the door handle with his left hand. His right one still held the Walther. The door wasn't locked, and the next moment, he had kicked it wide open.

Lemaitre's appearance—less than ten seconds after the ringing of the

132

alarm bell, barely two seconds after the shots—took Rocco and his men so totally by surprise that for an instant they were as motionless as a group in a waxworks tableau.

The hatchet men—there were two of them—were still standing over Orsini's body; they were still, in fact, leveling their guns at it, as though about to shoot again to make assurance doubly sure. Jack Rocco himself— a balding, effeminate-looking man in his late thirties, with cold, slate gray eyes—was standing behind them. Further back in the room, which was furnished as a small private bar, a fourth man was standing by a second door. He would be the soft-voiced manager, Ron Curtis, thought Lem, and that door probably gave on to a back staircase, which in turn gave straight on to the street. The perfect getaway route—only none of them would be using it now; if it cost him his life, he would make sure of that.

It was as though Lem was suddenly imbued with Orsini's brand of fury. He scarcely recognized his own voice as he shouted at the two hatchet men: "Drop those guns, laddies, or *you'll* be getting it through the forehead, or better still, between the eyes . . ."

His hatred of them was so intense that he was almost disappointed when, literally gaping, they allowed their guns to clatter to the floor.

Only Jack Rocco spoke, his high-pitched voice a grating sneer.

"So, just one nosy policeman is enough to scare you! Don't you realize we outnumber him four to one?"

"Try anything on, any of you—" Lemaitre's voice was almost shaking with anger, "—and you'll find out quick just how much good that'll do you!"

Partly to emphasize the point, and partly to halt Ron Curtis, whom he saw out of the corner of his eye was sidling toward the farther door, Lem fired the Walther twice.

A lot of things happened almost simultaneously.

Two bullets thwacked into the wall an inch above Curtis's head. He started back with a choking cry. From out in the street came the sound of a police car pulling up, its siren wailing. Jack Rocco's face turned a dirty gray.

Lemaitre followed Rocco's eyes and suddenly understood Jack's feelings exactly.

Dino Orsini was moving.

"SO ALL I can say, Gee-Gee, is handsome apologies and full marks to the bloody major."

Lemaitre was almost babbling into the telephone, but Gideon did not try to slow him down. To hear someone light-headed with relief, rushing out a tale of triumph, was just the tonic he needed on this most strenuous of days.

"You remember what he told us," Lemaitre chatted on.

" *'Gunmen instinctively go for the body first.'* How right he was. Rocco's two choice specimens followed that instinct, in direct defiance of their boss's orders. You can understand it, of course. You'd have to be a hundred degrees subhuman to be able to shoot a man between the eyes when he's actually standing there, staring at you. Far easier to aim lower, at the chest or stomach, and leave the head shots, as a kind of coup de grace, to be pumped in later, when the victim's already ninety percent dead.

"Their body shots, fired at point-blank range, hit the iron raincoat so hard that Dino was paralyzed with shock. Probably he also lost consciousness. He certainly dropped like a stone. I'd have heard his breathing in my ear, of course, but the lapel-mike got smashed in the fall and went dead. Looking back, I'm amazed I didn't notice the absence of blood around his body, but—"

"You had one or two other things to take care of, from what you've told me," Gideon said drily.

Lemaitre grunted. "The gunmen themselves weren't entirely convinced that they'd killed him. They were about to fire again when I burst in on them and they probably *would* have aimed for the head this time. As the major said, 'The third or fourth shots may be aimed higher, but by that time there will be—'"

"'Distracting action by the bodyguard,'" Gideon finished, chuckling. "Intentionally or otherwise, you certainly supplied that—and at *very* great personal risk. I'm going to see that that's not forgotten, Lem."

"All part of the service, Gee-Gee," Lemaitre said lightly, but a certain tremor in his voice betrayed how moved he was by the tribute.

More briskly, Gideon went on, "Incidentally, where's Orsini now?"

"In bed, cherishing his bruises, being nursed by a tearful Vittoria and all five of his bambinos," said Lemaitre. "Finchley is manning the stakeout across the road from his restaurant, just in case Rocco's got any stray henchmen still on the prowl. But I imagine Dino's safe enough. So much of the evidence against Rocco is in the can, where no bullets can wipe it out."

134

"Don't jump to conclusions," Gideon said sharply. "Taped evidence isn't usually accepted in court. Though in this case the mob was caught so red-handed that I imagine an exception might be made."

"Rocco imagines that, too," Lem said grimly. "I've had one interview with him in his cell already, and he was singing so hard that even his lawyer was deafened."

Gideon burst out laughing as he replaced the receiver, feeling happier than he had done for weeks.

It was to be many hours before he would know such an anxiety-free moment again.

He glanced at his watch, and saw that it was nearly half-past four; and he had not even completed the first draft of his report to Scott-Marle. It was certainly nowhere near the dictating stage. He had not yet "wanted—er, required" Sabrina at all, he told himself, with a fleeting grin that perhaps held a hint of regret.

Until Lem's telephone call, it had been a depressingly, perhaps ominously, negative afternoon.

There had been little or nothing untoward to report on the Wellesley Estate front. Riddell had telephoned to say that tonight's Gideon's Force patrols were now organized in detail, the first two to leave the Wellesley substation at eight. Riddell added that he had interviewed Gerard Hopkins, who had remained vague and prevaricating over the list of schoolboy suspects. A man was now following him, but hadn't much to report; Hopkins had had a full timetable of teaching and had spent all day at Wellesley High School.

There had been an encouraging development at the hospital. Eric Beresford was showing the first signs of coming out of his coma. His heart was beating more strongly. They had decided against a second operation. He was still in the intensive care unit, Marjorie keeping vigil by his bed. Two uniformed constables were in constant guard outside the door. Since Eric was a key witness, there was always the possibility of an attack, a possibility that Riddell was the last man to overlook.

In another ward, Frank Fenton, alias John Rowlandes, was still being detained, officially "for observation." During visiting hour that morning, he had had several reporters and photographers around his bed. Gideon was furious when he heard this, not because he feared the publicity, but because the presence of the newsmen would have prevented Rowlandes

135

from having more interesting visitors. Perhaps they would come tonight. If not, he would have to review the situation. He couldn't keep a perfectly fit Rowlandes in hospital indefinitely . . .

Just then, the telephone rang. It was Kate, wanting to hear the latest news of Marjorie and Eric.

When Gideon had told her . . .

"I *must* go down to the hospital again and see them," she said. "The best time would be when the evening visiting hour starts at seven-thirty. Penny's going out somewhere, so I don't have to consider her. Could you possibly manage to be home by seven for supper, or shall I leave you something cold?"

"I'll be back, all being well," Gideon promised, and Kate rang off, surprised and delighted. He'd probably get on with that report faster, Gideon told himself, if he took it home. That is, if he was left in peace, but some sixth sense told him that it was going to be anything but a peaceful night.

Some sixth sense . . .

His thoughts switched abruptly to the Cargill kidnapping case. There again the afternoon had proved disquietingly negative. There had been no more leads from seaside resorts, and he had heard nothing from Matt since—

As if on cue, the door burst open and Matt Honiwell came in. It was a Honiwell Gideon had never seen before. His face had weariness and frustration written all over it, but there was also something deeper—an ironic bitterness that came close to savagery.

"You warned me about ESP wild-goose chases, George, and by gum, I wish I'd listened. I've just got proof positive that Brodnik is a charlatan. He has had us *all* on a wild-goose chase—right from the word go!"

136

16

No Such Place

"SIT DOWN, MATT," Gideon said sharply. "And calm down."

He did something that was unusual for him. He produced a bottle of whisky and poured Matt a stiff drink—and himself a mild one.

Matt sank down into a comfortable leather armchair and emptied half the glass at a gulp.

"I certainly needed that," he muttered. "Didn't realize that it showed."

"After a sleepless night and a day battling with the intangibles, you wouldn't be human if *something* didn't show," Gideon said. "Tethers aren't all that long. There comes a time when one gets to the end of them."

Watching Honiwell empty the rest of the glass, it suddenly struck him that Matt's hair looked perceptibly grayer than it had done at the start of the Cargill case, six weeks before. It was most probably a trick of the light; he hoped it was. Nothing took as much out of a police officer as a major kidnapping case, particularly one that ended in tragedy. And Matt was a little like Kate in one respect. He took the human side of things very hard.

Gideon finished his own whisky, and then said, briskly. "All right. Now just what's happened to make you change your attitude to Brodnik so completely?"

"I followed your hunch and rang the Bognor inspector," Matt began. "I told him to give full priority to the investigation of the constable's story. He put three men onto the job immediately; in two hours they'd tracked down and interviewed five local artists.

"One of them was an old boy of about seventy-eight. Name of Guthrie, Malcolm Guthrie. They showed him a radioed photostat of Brodnik's sketch, and he nearly jumped out of his skin. The sketch corresponded in every detail with a picture he had painted years ago—in 1933, to be precise.

"And when I say every detail, George, I mean every detail. The cottage halfway up the hill, the church with the crooked steeple, the rocks, the sea, the signpost pointing to a place beginning with the letters 'SW'—there can be no question of coincidence. Guthrie's picture *was* of Brodnik's scene.

"The men became very excited. All they had to do, they thought, was ask Guthrie to take them to the spot he'd painted. But there they ran into just a little difficulty." The savagely sardonic note was back in Matt's voice. "There is, quite simply, *no such place*. The picture was called 'Midsummer Day's Dream' and was intended to show an impossibly idyllic country view. Guthrie made the entire scene up out of his head! That church steeple is crooked because it was badly drawn in the first place. He left it like that because he thought it gave the picture its one touch of originality! There isn't even such a village as 'SW——.' The wording on the signpost was never completed, just left as a surrealistic squiggle.

"I talked to Guthrie on the telephone myself. He was rather proud of this particular picture. He had some success with it back in the early thirties. Dozens of framed reproductions were offered for sale. It appeared on calendars, biscuit tins, and for all I know, on chocolate boxes. I thought there was something chocolate-boxy about it when I first saw it!

"So it's obvious what's happened. Brodnik must have come across the picture at some time or other, perhaps on some item in a junk shop window. The picture somehow stuck in the back of his mind, and now it's suddenly surfaced as an ESP vision." Honiwell laughed, a strange, hard laugh. "And I've been fool enough to have half the police of the country looking out for a place that could only be found on a few old prints and biscuit tins!"

"A very few, I should think," Gideon said thoughtfully. "Forty odd years is a long time for artistic efforts of that kind to survive. There may not be more than one or two copies of that painting still in existence, in any form."

138

Matt shrugged. "What does it matter if there are one or two or twenty-two?" he asked.

Gideon remained thoughtful. His hand crept into his right-hand coat pocket and began fumbling with the bowl of his pipe.

"Matt," he said. "Something rather odd has struck me. Let's suppose you are the prisoner of a kidnapper. Let's suppose you are being shut up day and night in a small room—perhaps gagged and bound, perhaps kept docile by some kind of drug. And let's suppose that your mind, under extreme duress, suddenly develops the power to transmit an image telepathically.

"Now answer me this. What sort of image would your mind transmit? It couldn't send details about the location of the place where you're being held—*because you wouldn't know them.* You were probably brought in there unconscious or blindfolded. All you've ever done since your ordeal began is stare at the four bare walls of your prison.

"But if the walls aren't entirely bare . . . if, by some chance, a picture has been left on one of them . . . then common sense suggests that that is the very sort of image that, consciously or subconsciously, you might transmit."

Honiwell leaned forward.

"I thought you didn't believe such things were possible."

Gideon shrugged.

"As to that, I've had too many odd intuitions myself to swear positively one way or the other. In this case I think it's more probable that Brodnik did have a vision, than that he should be led astray by something he once saw in a junkshop."

Matt had slumped back in his chair, once again despairing.

"But still, where does that leave us? Now all we know about the kidnapper's hideout is that it may possibly have a certain picture on the wall! How the hell can we hope to track it down in time? Don't forget, according to Brodnik, we've only a few hours left at the most."

"Steady," Gideon said quietly. "Don't let's give up until we have to. We've already established that there are only likely to be one or two of these pictures about. And since Malcolm Guthrie is a Bognor artist, our best chances of finding one are in the Bognor area . . ."

Suddenly Gideon started, and in his excitement, actually brought the pipe out of his pocket and rapped with it on the desk top.

"... *where one was seen recently by a young constable.* I think it might be an idea to have a word with that man."

He reached for the telephone and asked to be put through to Bognor.

Matt was beginning to be infected by Gideon's excitement.

"He claimed he didn't remember where he saw it. But it ought to be possible to jog his memory."

"I should bloody well think it ought," Gideon said grimly. "No one's got any business being a police constable if he can't remember the precise location of things he—Hullo! This is Commander Gideon. I would like to speak to the detective inspector in charge, please."

Within a few minutes, Gideon had had the constable, a young man who rejoiced in the name of Thomas Watson-Wright, brought to the telephone. He arrived breathless and panting. He had been on point duty in a busy shopping street about two hundred yards from the police station; had been informed by walkie-talkie that Gideon wanted to speak to him, and had run back all the way.

He began by insisting that he had no idea where he had seen the painting, but his voice betrayed excessive nervousness, and Gideon wasn't conceited enough to believe that it could all be caused by talking to the head of the CID.

His voice rose to the famous Gideon roar.

"Look, Watson-Wright. By reporting this picture in the first place, you made what could be a crucial contribution to a major case. Now you're messing it up by withholding the one piece of information that really matters. If—as I suspect—you're doing it deliberately, then God help you! I'm going to ask you once—and only once—again. *Where did you see that picture?*"

There were not many men in the top echelons of Scotland Yard who could stand up to Gideon when he was in this mood. The young Bognor constable didn't even try. He began pouring out an embarrassed and somewhat incoherent story. Gideon listened in silence, then he thanked him surprisingly warmly before he replaced the receiver and turned to Matt.

"Apparently he saw the picture in a Bognor holiday bungalow that he rented for a week last year. It—the picture, I mean—was hanging in a back bedroom."

"What was all the secrecy about, then?"

140

Gideon grinned.

"He's having an affair with a policewoman. They spent the week in the bungalow together, and there'd be hell to pay if their respective section-house sergeants got to hear about it."

"But why didn't they pick somewhere farther away for a holiday love nest?"

Gideon shrugged then his expression became one of keen urgency as the importance of what he was about to say struck him.

"This particular bungalow is so secluded that they didn't have to. It stands well back in its own grounds. It is hidden from the road by thick pine trees. The neighboring bungalows are over a hundred yards away on each side. The place even has its own path down to the beach."

"My God," Matt said. "Do you realize that you've just described the perfect—"

"—kidnapper's hideout? Yes, I know." Tensely, Gideon reached out once again for the telephone. "The bungalow is known as Pine Corner, and the real estate agents who arranged Watson-Wright's booking are a firm called Small and Pearson. I'm going to ring them now and inquire if Pine Corner has been rented by the same person for the past six weeks . . ."

Three minutes later, Gideon had his answer.

"The bungalow was booked from the twenty-third of July to the sixteenth of September. The sum of £240 paid in advance."

There was a moment's silence while Matt and Gideon stared at each other, sharing a sense of rising excitement so intense that it seemed to crackle like an electric charge between them.

"Do you know what I'd do if I were you?" Gideon said at length. "I'd get hold of Cargill and Brodnik and drive down there with all possible speed. Meanwhile, I will see that the Bognor CID go to town on the tenant who booked it. I'll be very surprised if, by the time you've arrived, they haven't dug up enough suspicious facts to justify a search warrant."

"But suppose they haven't?" Matt said. "Will you back me if I decide on the spot to go ahead regardless?"

Remembering all that had gone before, Honiwell expected at best a grudging, hesitant reply; perhaps even another *volte face.*

But without the slightest hint of a pause, Gideon smiled and said, "Don't worry. This time the answer's '*Yes,* Matt.' Yes to you pulling all the stops out—all the way."

17

Visiting Hour

TWO HOURS LATER, another September twilight was beginning. It was a totally different one from the previous night's. Then, London had been awash in a surrealistic sea of color. Now, there seemed to be no color left anywhere in the world. A mass of iron-gray clouds hid the whole sky, bringing premature darkness and a hint of impending thunder. In some people this created a mood of unrest; in others it merely caused a deepening depression.

Gideon, having just seen Kate off to the hospital, was in the kitchen, washing up the few plates they had used during a hasty supper. He looked forward gloomily to an evening alone in the house, struggling with that report for Scott-Marle.

Excitement, tinged with disquiet, was the dominant mood on the Wellesley Estate. In a dozen different houses, their owners were getting ready to set out for the police station, to report for patrol duty sharp at eight. In two dozen other houses, people were telling themselves that they must forget about TV and try to snatch some sleep. They were the personnel scheduled to report for the later shifts, between midnight and dawn.

Everywhere on the Estate the talk was of Gideon's Force. It had brought the first night of peace in two long and weary months, and with it, the first real hope that the lawlessness might have been conquered at last.

But not everybody's face lit up when the Force was mentioned. Some of them, mostly teenagers, and young teenagers at that, grew sullen and angry, and worried their parents with defiant looks that said clearly enough: "Wait and see."

In the Wellesley police substation, Tom Riddell was staring out of the window at the gathering darkness, more worried than any of the parents. At this rate, it was likely to be pretty dark well before eight; and so many lights on the Estate had been vandalized that on almost every street there would be pools of shadow. If the enemy wanted to attack the members of the patrols while they were walking to the police station, conditions would be ideal. Riddell decided to play safe and see that all patrol men and women were collected by area car.

In the Fulton North General Hospital, just beyond the borders of the Estate, Kate Gideon was as anxious as Tom Riddell, but for different reasons. She was standing talking to Marjorie Beresford, who had come to the door of the intensive care unit in response to her tap on the glass. Through this glass, which enclosed the unit as completely as though it were a giant goldfish bowl, Kate could just glimpse a deathly pale Eric.

"He's getting more color now, don't you think?" Marjorie said, with pathetic eagerness.

There was not a vestige of color discernible on the boy's face, but Kate could not do anything but agree, as enthusiastically as possible.

"He's talking quite a bit, too," Marjorie went on. "Not making much sense, though. He seems to be saying Mr. Gideon's name over and over again . . ."

At that moment, Eric turned over and started muttering something. Marjorie flew back to his bedside. Kate tried to go with her, but a nurse barred the way.

"Only parents are allowed inside I'm afraid—"

The nurse broke off. Eric was suddenly sitting up, wide-eyed with terror; it was exactly as though he could still see his attackers, was still pleading with them for his life.

"I shan't tell Gideon anything, I swear I won't. You can't blame me just because he came to my place! My Mum called him, I'll bet. She knows the Gideons personally, see? It's her fault . . . all her fault . . . and theirs . . ."

If Marjorie had not herself been under sedation, she would surely have

144

broken down. As it was, the remorse on her face was terrible. Kate could only look away, appalled at the realization that the cost of knowing the Gideons could come so very, very high.

In Ward 3B, two corridors away from the intensive care unit, Frank Fenton, alias the young Detective Constable John Rowlandes, was feeling anything but remorseful. He had just glanced up and seen three faces that filled him with the purest joy.

They belonged to three members of the street gang that he had "joined" the night before.

So the enemy had swallowed the bait at last, Rowlandes told himself. It had all been worth while, his embarrassing twenty-four hours of pretending to be in agony from an almost painless head and noticeably unbroken jaw . . .

He grinned, then remembered to wince as though at a sudden spasm.

"Hi, fellers. Thought you were never going to show up."

They edged forward, awkwardly, to his bedside.

"Hi, Frank," their leader said. "We'd 'ave come sooner, only the gentlemen of the press was 'ere."

"Treating you like a blooming 'ero, from the look of it," one of his companions added.

"As you deserve, Frank," finished the third. "Seeing you take on Mr. Effing Pig Gideon last night was the biggest treat we've had in years."

Rowlandes turned his grin into a grimace.

"He effing well got his own back on me, though, the bastard. I barely touched him, and look what he did to me."

"Look what he's doing to all of us, with his bloody Gideon's Force," the leader said. "Every square foot of the Estate is crawling with coppers and coppers' narks from eight o'clock till morning." Then he dropped his voice to a whisper. "Won't be for long, though. You can be sure of that."

Rowlandes, leaning his elbow against his pillow, responded in the same excited whisper.

"We're going to hit back? How? Where?"

There was an odd silence. Blast! thought Rowlandes, he'd been too eager with his questions; had overplayed his hand. He contorted his face into another spasm of agony and burst out angrily:

"Aren't I entitled to know *anything*—after all I've been through?"

145

That was when the leader made the strangest, perhaps the most revealing, remark of the evening.

"Take it easy, Frank. We can't tell you what we don't know ourselves. *We're* all too old to be in tonight's caper. You've got to be wet behind the ears to be allowed a piece of the real action."

Rowlandes wondered if he'd heard right. These three all looked to be somewhere between seventeen and nineteen, hardly in their dotage. What were they saying, then? That in this gang, the really rough stuff was *literally left to children*?

But why? What sort of leadership would entrust the most dangerous work to thirteen- or fifteen-year-olds, when there were youths of eighteen and nineteen only too anxious to do it?

He could make no sense of it.

But Rowlandes had no time to pursue his thoughts.

The leader was bending over him, whispering again.

"This much I can tell you, though. There are going to be two Gideon's Force patrols setting out from the fuzz-bin at eight o'clock tonight. And if the kiddie winkies don't muff it—*only one will be coming back.*"

IT WAS A good ten minutes after that when Rowlandes's guests left him. The young DC looked at his watch and saw that it was already a quarter to eight. He slipped out of bed, not even waiting to put a dressing gown over his pajamas, and moved down the ward into the nurses' room.

Two nurses giggled nervously when he came in. They knew he was a mystery patient, pretending to be ill for police purposes. They had also seen his picture in the papers. He represented glamour in a big way.

They stopped giggling as they saw the tense, scared look in his eyes.

Yes, of course he could use the telephone . . .

Rowlandes dialed the police station and in a moment was telling Riddell all that he had learned.

The time was now ten to eight. Outside the police station the area car had just drawn up with the first consignment of patrol personnel. It included Harold Neame, the Wellesley High School headmaster; Mr. Suncliffe, vicar of All Saints, Wellesley; and Mrs. Sylvia Thompson, a councilor and prominent women's lib campaigner.

As Tom Riddell watched them being ushered through the station doorway he felt sweat breaking out on his forehead.

Lambs to the slaughter, he told himself, repeating the phrase he had used the night before.

They were all lambs to the slaughter . . . unless he could get through to Gideon and obtain his authority to cancel the eight o'clock patrols. It wasn't something he dared to do on his own.

He reached for the telephone and dialed Gideon's home number.

During the next five minutes he dialed it over and over again . . . but all he could hear was the engaged signal.

Gideon was usually pretty short with everybody on the telephone. Who on earth could be detaining him for this infuriating length of time?

In point of fact, the culprit was Matt Honiwell, reporting from Bognor police station, where he had just arrived with Gordon Cargill and Jacob Brodnik.

"While we were driving down, the local CID did a superb job checking up on the tenant who took the bungalow. And I don't think there's any reasonable doubt that he's our man. His name is Leonard Lacey, by the way, and he was seen to arrive at Pine Corner, late at night, on July 28—just a few hours after Barbara's kidnapping! During the next week or so, on several occasions, three other men were seen with him—"

"Members of the kidnap gang," Gideon suggested.

"Probably. But whoever they were, they went away. Since very early in August, Lacey seems to have lived at Pine Corner alone. But not quite alone, according to one neighbor, Mrs. Masters, a sharp-eyed old lady of eighty. Mrs. M. swears that on one occasion she saw a girl's face at the back bedroom window. She couldn't be sure—her house is a hundred yards away and her eyesight isn't too good—so she didn't report it to the police. Neither did she report a scream, coming from the direction of Pine Corner, which once woke her up at one A.M. It could have been a late-night horror film on TV; there was one showing at the time.

"There are a lot of other items I could mention. It seems that Lacey has an almost pathological objection to being spied on and never leaves the premises. He has milk, bread, and groceries delivered at the door—"

"Never mind all that," Gideon barked. "You've obviously got enough

147

evidence to get your search warrant, and even to hold Lacey for questioning. When are you going to start for Pine Corner?"

"Straight away," Matt said. "Apart from Cargill and Brodnik, I'm taking Constable Watson-Wright, because he knows the house, and two detective sergeants, both armed."

"*And* you'll need them," Gideon said. "Let's face it. If Barbara Cargill is alive, that means that Lacey has been standing close guard over her, all by himself, for more than a month. To do that, he's got to be a psycho. Or if he wasn't one at the beginning, he'll have turned into one by now. So there's no sense in taking chances. He could do literally anything—to Barbara, to himself, or to any of you."

"I'm not worried about what he may do," Matt said shortly. "I'm more worried about what he may have already done."

There was a new note in Matt's voice. A note of dread.

"Yes?"

"There's one thing I haven't told you. Mrs. Masters claims that Lacey was out in the garden of Pine Corner at about five o'clock this afternoon. She couldn't see much through the pines, but she got the impression that he was chopping up something with an axe. Then later she smelled bonfire smoke."

Gideon was beginning to feel uneasy too, but there was no point in showing it.

"People burn rubbish when they're thinking of leaving a place," he said reassuringly. "Perhaps Lacey's just getting ready to clear out."

"Possibly," Matt said. "Only it so happens that half an hour earlier, at around four-thirty, Brodnik was trying to get a signal from Barbara Cargill.

"For a moment he 'saw' the cottage scene, much more faintly than usual. Then suddenly there was a kind of cut out. The scene went dark, and there has been no signal since. Putting these two things together—"

"The only things you ought to be putting together," Gideon snapped, "are Lacey's wrists and a pair of handcuffs. Concentrate on that, Matt, and don't get morbid until you're compelled to. Get going—there's not a moment to lose."

He sounded brisk and bracing; it was what Matt needed. But inside him a glacial mixture of eeriness and foreboding seemed to be turning his blood into a sluggish-moving jelly.

148

He replaced the receiver slowly, and his fingers were still in contact with it when the telephone rang again.

This time it was Riddell, recounting everything that Rowlandes had heard from his visitors and urgently requesting permission to cancel both of the eight o'clock patrols.

Gideon's blood no longer felt as though it was congealing. Anger seemed to send it roaring through his veins at twice the usual rate.

"What—and leave the whole Estate at the mercy of these murderous 'kiddiewinkies'?" he roared. "That's totally out of the question. As you ought to have the bloody well *known* it would be before you rang!"

The moment he had said that, Gideon's anger abated. He remembered a sentence he had just been writing in his report to Scott-Marle, a sentence he had included with Riddell in mind, but with which he was nonetheless in wholehearted agreement.

"Since the Force consists of untrained civilian volunteers, great care must be taken to see that they are never unnecessarily put at risk."

But surely that did not—could not—mean that the patrols should stay at home at the first hint of danger?

Suddenly he had an idea that came as an answer both to the problem and to his underlying sense of restlessness, his basic urge for action.

"I'll tell you what you *can* do," he said slowly. "You can hold back those patrols for a quarter of an hour, while we make sure that they're fully protected . . . *and* suitably augmented."

"Augmented?"

"That's right, Tom." There was now no mistaking the excitement in Gideon's voice. "In a quarter of an hour, I can be with you, and I'll take a place in one of the patrols myself. I suggest you draw a revolver out of stores and join the other one. If we've got to send lambs to the slaughter, the least we can do is see that they're adequately led."

18

Murderer Manqué

ON THE SOUTH Coast the daylight lingers just a little longer than in London. By eight o'clock on the Wellesley Estate, everything was dark, but at Bognor Regis, a pale gray sky still brooded over a misty blue sea.

Against this sky, the silhouettes of the conifers that gave Pine Corner its name reared stark and chilling. They certainly guaranteed seclusion, Matt Honiwell thought grimly. Not a single brick of the bungalow could be seen through them, nor a gleam of light from any of its windows.

The crowded police car—Honiwell, Watson-Wright, and a detective sergeant driver occupied the front seat; Gordon Cargill, Brodnik, and the second detective sergeant were at the rear—turned from the main road into the private lane that ran past the side of the bungalow down to the beach.

"Pull in here," Honiwell ordered. The sergeant behind the wheel nodded, pulled to the side of the lane, and stopped.

Matt glanced at Watson-Wright.

"There is a gate along here, you said?"

"That's right, sir. What they'd have called a 'tradesmen's entrance' in the old days. There's a path on the other side that winds around to the back door. But if you want the front door, you've only got to turn off the path just before you get to the house, walk across a patch of lawn between two pampas bushes, and you're there."

151

Matt nodded.

"These pampas bushes—are they thick?"

"Very, sir. At least, they were last year when I was . . . er . . . here."

The two detective sergeants grinned at each other. Watson-Wright's youthful cheeks took on a deeper hue. He was a fair-skinned, easily flustered type; the last man, going by appearances, who ought to have picked a police career. Yet he had been prompt in remembering and reporting that picture, more prompt than many another constable would have been in his place. So one never knew . . .

"Anyone hiding behind one of those bushes would be concealed from the front door?" Matt asked.

"I'd certainly say so, sir, yes."

"Right. Then here's what I suggest we do. Mr. Cargill, you, sergeant"—he indicated the driver—"and I will go in at this gate and walk around to the front door. You"—he indicated the sergeant in the back seat—"and Watson-Wright follow and conceal yourselves behind the pampas until we have got Lacey talking. Then I want you to make for the back of the house and peer through the windows—especially the back bedroom ones. You've brought torches, I hope?" They nodded. "If you find a window that's heavily curtained and can't be opened without smashing the glass, come around to the front and report it to me . . . Okay?"

Everyone in the car chorused assent, except for Brodnik, who had been given no instructions and didn't seem to expect any. The ESP expert—looking old, slight, and frail in the near-darkness—sat quietly, staring out of the window toward those towering pines. It was as if the trees had a message for him; a message he would rather not have heard.

His hand on the inside door handle, Matt suddenly realized he'd forgotten Brodnik. He swung around to the old man.

"Will you be all right waiting here? Of course, if you'd rather accompany Mr. Cargill, the sergeant, and me to the front door, you can. I just thought that if there was any rough stuff—"

"I'd be in the way?" Brodnik smiled faintly. "You're right, Mr. Honiwell. I probably would be. I shall just sit here and pray that my part in the proceedings isn't . . . still to come."

For a moment, Matt didn't grasp his meaning. But Gordon Cargill did and let out a stifled groan of combined dismay and despair. Of course, Matt thought: Brodnik was by profession a *corpse-diviner*.

He shuddered, a sound that seemed to be taken up mockingly by the trees, as a sudden zephyr from the sea started a hundred thousand pine needles swaying and rustling above their heads.

"For God's sake, Matt," Gordon breathed, "let's get going!"

His voice sounded as dry as the rustling needles.

Matt nodded and opened the door. A couple of seconds later he had negotiated a creaking gate and was leading Gordon and one of the detective sergeants up the winding path through the Pine Corner garden. It was getting too dark to see very much, and what light was left was lost in the dense shadow of the pines. He couldn't just make out the low silhouette of the bungalow and the two areas of misty-gray in front of it, which he took to be the pampas bushes. Suddenly his nostrils caught a whiff of woodsmoke, and he remembered the report of the afternoon's bonfire.

No time to think about that now, he told himself, and quickened his pace. A moment later, he was brushing past the pampas bushes. Almost at once he found himself on a verandah, facing the bungalow's front door.

The top half of the door was made of colored glass, through which a weird pink light was streaming.

Matt glanced over his shoulder, and saw that Gordon and the sergeant were right behind him. A rustling from the direction of the pampas bushes told him that Watson-Wright and the other sergeant were in their concealed positions.

He swung back to the door and pressed a button bell push.

Nothing happened, so he pressed it again.

He kept his hand on it for a long time before footsteps sounded on the other side, and the door was opened.

The man who opened it had his back to the light. He was in his shirtsleeves and his left sleeve was rolled up.

On the exposed arm, there was something that caught the light . . . a bead of blood, as though he had given himself an injection.

Christ, Matt thought. What have we here—a psycho and a junkie combined?

One thing was certain. No one normal would have stood, silently staring, as this man did.

And there was nothing normal about his voice when he spoke. It was weak and quavering, and once having started, babbled on.

"You're . . . you're the police, aren't you? I saw you . . . watched you

153

coming up the path from the back gate. Five of you, I counted . . . Where are the others? Gone around the back, to spy?"

"That's right," Matt said quietly. "You have sharp eyes, Lacey."

"Sharp eyes . . . sharp brain . . . sharp everything," Lacey burbled, and began to laugh. "Only one thing I lack, really . . . *nerve.*"

He held up his left arm and stroked away the bead of blood.

"When I saw you coming I knew I'd never get away. I'm too unsteady on my legs, you see. Haven't . . . haven't eaten anything much for days. . . . So I've just given myself a shot of morphine. It should have been a fatal dose . . . All . . . all I had to do was press home the plunger. But . . . but I couldn't do it. Any more than I could ever do it . . . to *her* . . ."

"You're talking about Barbara Cargill, I take it?" Matt said. "In that case Leonard Lacey, it is my duty to arrest you—"

"For her murder? Oh, no. *That* you can never get me for. She's dying from completely natural causes—"

"Dying?" The use of the present participle galvanized Gordon Cargill out of his numb despair. "You mean—you mean she's not—"

A loud rustling from the pampas bushes interrupted them. Watson-Wright came crashing through, up to the verandah, his face red with excitement.

"I flashed my torch through one of the back bedroom windows. There's a girl in there, lying on the bed. I thought she was dead at first, but when the torch flashed on her face, she blinked, tried to sit up . . ."

Gordon thrust Lacey aside as effortlessly as if he were a dummy and made for the back of the hall. There were two doors leading off. Some instinct seemed to tell him which one to choose. He hurled open the right-hand one, and switched on the light. Then he went into the room, out of sight of the hall.

Nobody moved. Lacey had been thrown against a hall table. He stayed there, leaning heavily against it, sweat pouring off him, strength leaving him as the strong shot of morphine took effect. Watson-Wright, the detective sergeant, and Matt remained on the porch, standing stock still, straining to catch the slightest sound from that bedroom . . .

The first sound that came wasn't slight. It was a half-hysterical sobbing.

Honiwell's heart turned over when he realized that *two voices were making it—a man's and a girl's.* So Watson-Wright hadn't exaggerated. Barbara was alive and not only alive, but conscious . . .

Matt's relief was so great that everything seemed to reel around him.

A sound from Lacey sobered him: a strange sound that was halfway between a scream and a giggle.

The morphine was rapidly reducing Lacey to the state in which he'd kept Barbara Cargill for six cruel weeks. A state of weakness, dizziness, high delirium.

He sank heavily into a chair beside the hall table. The light was shining fully on him for the first time, showing him to be a smallish man of about forty. He might once have been considered darkly handsome, but there wasn't much that was handsome about him now. His face reflected his fever and shone with sweat, emphasizing a weak, quivering mouth. Words came from it, now loud, now sinking to a whisper, in an incoherent jumble.

"So Barbara's won. Why wouldn't she die? It was asking too much of me. I . . . I couldn't kill her outright. It was mean of her . . . *mean.*"

Then came what was, for Matt, the sickest moment of the whole case. Leonard Lacey's face suddenly took on a look of half-crazy, wholly evil pride.

"I thought I'd won this afternoon, though," he said brightly. "I propped her up on her pillow so that she could see me through the window . . . and then I went down the garden and made a bonfire out of something she'd taken a great fancy to. Something, in fact, that almost seemed to be keeping her alive.

"A bloody silly *picture* . . ."

Within two hours, Matt was well on the way to tying up the whole of the Cargill kidnapping case. Leonard Lacey's self-injected shot of morphine had the same effect on his brain as a truth drug. He babbled the frankest answers to all Matt's questions; describing in detail the whole kidnapping plot and unhesitatingly giving the names of his three associates. Ten minutes' telephoning to London, and Matt had started the process that was to end with the capture of them all. Lacey also revealed how he obtained his supplies of morphine: once a doctor, he still had friends in the medical profession, who, imagining him to be an addict, prescribed for him.

A full confession having been dictated, Lacey was taken, handcuffed, to Bognor police station. With Gordon in attendance, Barbara had long before been driven in an ambulance to the Bognor War Memorial Hospital. There she was found to be suffering from shock, nervous exhaustion, near-starvation, and the effects of six weeks of morphine overdosing.

"Any other woman would be dead by now," a baffled doctor said. "A strange thing, the will to survive."

When Matt looked in to see her, Barbara was propped up in bed. She was a slight, red-haired girl in her early twenties, with large, gray green eyes; and although her face was deathly white, and her eyes were deeply sunken, there was a newly awakened aura of life about her. She was holding her husband's hand, and when both of them tried huskily to express their thanks, Matt hurriedly excused himself.

There had been times when this case had nearly broken him. It was somehow fitting that it should end by showing him just how *un*breakable human beings could be.

SINCE GORDON WAS booking into a hotel at Bognor to be as close as he could to his wife, Matt found himself, at around ten o'clock, driving back to London with only Jacob Brodnik for company. He found the ESP man very poor company indeed.

"An unforgivable error on my part," he kept saying. "To have imagined that a subject was dead simply because *the object she was transmitting* was destroyed . . . ach, a schoolboy beginner would not make such a mistake! All the time, I must have been receiving a clear life signal, but my baffled mind chose to ignore it; to insist, in its confusion, that all was dark. I can only offer Mr. Cargill and you my sincere apologies."

"Which, so far as I am concerned, will not be accepted," Matt told him. "You don't seem to realize, Mr. Brodnik, that had it not been for you, nothing could have stopped the Cargill case from ending in tragedy. When the facts of your achievement get out, I believe it could mark a turning point in the whole story of ESP. Here, for once, is evidence strong enough to convince the most confirmed skeptic—"

Matt broke off, aware of Brodnik's twisted smile.

"Evidence, Mr. Honiwell? What evidence is there left to convince anyone of anything? The picture was totally destroyed in that bonfire. I doubt if either Lacey or Mrs. Cargill will have more than a blurred memory of it by the morning.

"In the end, the records will state that the police were led to Pine Corner by the purest chance. It *may* be added that one, Jacob Brodnik, gave some sort of help at some stage in the inquiry. But, I assure you, there will be nothing more."

"Well, let me assure *you,*" said Matt, "that there will be a great deal more in everything I say to the newspapers about this case. And I know that goes for Commander Gideon too."

"Commander Gideon . . . ye-es. From what you tell me, the successful ending of this case owes most of all to that very open-minded man. I hope—"

Honiwell glanced around as Brodnik broke off. The old man was peering fearfully through the windscreen. It was as though he could see much more than what was really there: a country road at night, swept by driving rain.

"You hope what?" Matt demanded.

Brodnik smiled self-deprecatingly. He might have been about to apologize for some awkward personal idiosyncrasy.

"I sometimes get strange, sudden anxieties about people . . . a sense that they are in danger, or facing a serious crisis. I have that feeling very strongly at this moment about Commander Gideon. I am just hoping that he will be all right."

Matt attempted one of his reassuring grins; but he was too conscious of who and what his passenger was. His lips simply wouldn't obey his order to smile, and he looked almost as fearful as Brodnik as he said, fervently, "I am just hoping so, too."

19

Ambush

FROM THE MOMENT he started patrolling the Wellesley Estate, Gideon's excitement at the project started fading, and he found himself very close to the mood of desperation and frustration that had overtaken Riddell. The curious atmosphere of the place, those rows and rows of identical buildings, with a hint of something evil lurking around every corner, began to get as deeply under his skin as it so obviously had done under Tom's. Suddenly, *he* was uneasy about the whole concept of Gideon's Force and fearful for the safety of its members—especially the six who were with him on this patrol.

One of them was Harold Neame, the headmaster who had started the whole vigilante movement and then become the Force's leading supporter. Another was the Reverend Hugh Suncliffe, the local vicar. A third was Mrs. Thompson, J.P. and Labour councillor. The remaining three were a bus conductor, a milkman, and a young woman librarian.

They had all been told, at the outset, that there were special risks involved in tonight's patrol: they would have guessed as much, anyway, from the fact that the commander of the CID was leading them. Far from being deterred, they had shown almost excessive enthusiasm and a confidence in his leadership that Gideon found more than a little disturbing.

"So this is it, is it?" Harold Neame had said, his steel-gray eyes glittering

159

with excitement. "The moment of truth, of confrontation, with the enemy. I thank whatever powers that be that I haven't missed it."

"I entirely agree, Mr. Neame," Mrs. Thompson asserted authoritatively. "Though I should hardly have put it in those words, I, too, consider it an honor to be here."

The milkman, an Irishman, had put it rather less conventionally.

"When I volunteered to join Gideon's Force, I'd never thought to be walkin' into battle behind the great man himself. It's a story I'll be tellin' till me dying day, even if that happens to be tonight."

The young librarian gave a gasp of alarm, which the bus conductor seized as an opportunity to put his arm protectively, or otherwise, around her shoulders.

"Don't worry, girlie. Nothing bad is going to happen to any of us. Not with Mr. Gideon coming all the way from Scotland Yard to make sure that it don't. Isn't that right, Mr. G.?"

Gideon studied them with a little less than enthusiasm. The girl librarian couldn't be more than eighteen; the vicar less than seventy; Harold Neame could prove to be more than tiresome. And these were the frontline troops he was wheeling out against a deadly enemy, known to be especially dangerous tonight! He decided to play it straight with them. It was the least he could do.

"No, that's not entirely right. I'm here to lead you, not protect you. All my presence guarantees is that you'll have a pair of sharp eyes at your service—and a trained police mind accustomed to emergencies. I also have a revolver, which may be of some use in certain circumstances. I'm providing truncheons to any of you who want one. And we are doubling the usual number of area cars on duty for the period of this patrol. There will be four of them circling the Estate constantly. I shall remain in continual walkie-talkie touch and insure that one of those cars is never more than thirty seconds away from our patrol."

"There you are, ducks." The bus conductor squeezed the librarian's hand. "Told you, didn't I? We couldn't possibly be safer."

Gideon went on stonily, "The crucial fact remains, however, that if we're ambushed, a lot can happen in thirty seconds. Your safety will depend on the speed with which you obey my orders—and on a few other factors, including luck. I can't deny you'd be safer if you stayed at home."

160

It was then that the vicar made the speech that silenced them all.

"But, Mr. Gideon," he said quietly, "we *are* at home! It's just that our home, this Estate, has become the most dangerous place in England. And until we know why—what this inexplicable force is that is turning our children into thugs and murderers—there will soon be no question of safety for any of us, in any house, on any street. So no more talking, please, about danger. Just lead the way."

The patrol had set out five minutes later. By two minutes past nine it had completed its first circuit of the Estate, by nine thirty-six, its second. Riddell's patrol, following the same route but in the opposite direction, had passed them twice on each circuit.

Riddell saluted smartly every time the patrols came within sight of each other; but Gideon wasn't deceived. Tom was far too good a police officer to betray anxiety in the presence of a patrol he was leading; he would have kept his inner tensions under the firmest possible control.

At one meeting point, Tom came across to talk to Gideon; and at close quarters, it was obvious that he had lost none of his misgivings. It showed in the stiffness of his manner, the abruptness of his voice.

"There's—something I should have mentioned earlier," he said, his voice as toneless as an automaton. "When you go down Naughton Avenue, you might notice a man loitering about in the region of No. 14."

"A tall, lanky chap, about thirty, wearing a battered old raincoat?"

Ordinarily, Riddell would have grinned and said. "I might have known you'd have spotted him already." Tonight he just nodded stiffly.

"That's the man," he said. "I just thought I'd explain that he's there under my orders. No. 14 is Gerard Manley Hopkins's home, and he's the tail that's been following Hopkins all day. Waste of time, really. Hopkins went straight from the high school to his home and has stayed there ever since."

One consequence of Riddell's abruptness was that his voice was louder than usual, and carried farther than he had intended.

Harold Neame leaned forward.

"Do I understand that my English master is under police surveillance?" he inquired sharply. "Surely, you don't seriously suspect him of—"

"Mr. Hopkins," Riddell explained with obvious patience, "is being watched for his own protection. He was viciously attacked outside his home last night by a razor gang. We have reason to believe that he is in some danger of being attacked again."

"But I thought *we* were supposed to be the target for tonight," the Irish milkman said.

"*This* gang," Riddell said, his patience reinforced by an effort all could see, "*this* gang has often carried out multiple attacks simultaneously, sometimes as many as six in one night."

"But how can they do that *now*?" the Irishman protested. "With a dozen of us patrollin' around and around until we're dizzy, and police cars charging up and down every other minute, a man can hardly walk ten yards through the Estate without being spotted as a suspicious character. How can a *gang* of men possibly go anywhere?"

The bus conductor grunted.

"You're forgetting something, mate. We're not dealing with men, but with kids, kids who know this Estate like their own backyards. They can slip through holes in fences, clamber over roofs, cut across back gardens; there's no end to what the little bleeders can do, patrols or no patrols! Sometimes I wonder if they haven't got us at their mercy, after all!"

For a moment he had forgotten the librarian, whom he had been cheering up all through the evening. It seemed that she couldn't do without his support. Her voice rose dangerously, "In that case, why don't they attack and have done with it? Why do they stay hidden and . . . and do nothing, for hour after—"

Mrs. Thompson boomed her way into the conversation.

"There's one very probable answer to that, my dear. They could have hurriedly canceled their plans, once they saw that we had George Gideon with us."

Gideon expected this to be greeted with laughter. He was stunned when everyone in the patrol not only took the suggestion dead seriously, but seemed to be greatly heartened by it.

Embarrassment made his own voice abrupt, as he turned to Riddell. "Well, let's get on, shall we? It's gone ten o'clock, and both our patrols are behind time."

Riddell nodded and returned to his group, which started walking to the right. Gideon and his patrol turned to the left.

As they did so, there was a flash of lightning, followed by a rumble of thunder; at the same time, a drizzle of rain began, which was to continue for the rest of the night.

At that very moment, forty miles away on the Bognor—London road, Jacob Brodnik was staring into driving rain, and "seeing" Gideon facing a crisis and danger.

Gideon himself was aware only that vague misgivings at the back of his mind were, for some reason, suddenly solidifying.

They had turned into Naughton Avenue. There, halfway down the street as he expected, was the lanky young man in the battered mackintosh, the tail whose job it was to loiter outside No. 14.

But something was wrong. The man wasn't loitering. He was walking very fast, almost running, toward them.

"Sir," he said breathlessly, on arrival. "My name's Stanhope—detective constable. I'm supposed to be keeping an eye on—"

"Mr. Gerard Manley Hopkins. Yes, I know," Gideon said. "What's happened?"

"It's not what's happened, sir, it's what's happening," Stanhope said. "There is a continuous rustling sound . . . like feet moving through long grass. And it seems to be coming from the back of No. 14."

GIDEON GLOWERED.

"*Seems* to be coming? Haven't you taken a look?"

"There's no way to see the back of 14 from the front, sir. The garage and a side gate block one's view completely. I've tried the side gate and it's bolted. I was just going to knock at the front door and warn Mr. Hopkins when I saw you."

"Right," Gideon said. He was now speaking as softly as the other. "Which is No. 14? Can you point it out to me from here?"

"Yes, sir. It's three houses along, on the right. You can just see the garage—it's got one of these flat concrete roofs . . ."

Gideon's eyes followed Stanhope's pointing finger.

That was when he realized that something very strange was going on. It was hard to be sure—the drizzle kept getting into his eyes, and the night was so black that there was only the faintest hint of a skyline—but he didn't seem to be staring *only* at a garage roof. There was something rearing above

163

it, a silhouette—no, *four,* silhouettes—just the smallest degree blacker than the sky . . .

Gideon reached for his walkie-talkie. "This looks like it—the ambush," he whispered, with all the urgency at his command. "All cars at once, please, to 14 Naughton Avenue." He slipped the instrument back into his breast pocket, and then, raising his voice as far as he dared, called over his shoulder, "Back. Everybody—back . . ."

Everybody backed all right; but not at the same speed. The milkman collided with the bus conductor. The librarian screamed. The vicar tripped in his haste and fell against a fence. Mrs. Thompson cried out in anger as the headmaster tried to hustle her along.

"Mr. Neame, will you *kindly—*"

The words died in her throat as one of the figures on the garage roof switched on a powerful torch that caught the whole patrol in its beam. Almost simultaneously, the three other figures came to life and started firing. Gideon saw three flashes in quick succession, and heard, to his utter horror, not the *phwatt* of airguns but the roar of full-scale, medium-caliber revolvers.

A bullet, intended perhaps for Gordon, caught Stanhope. His lanky body spun around like a leaf in a gale as he fell heavily against a gate. It swung open, and he ended up face downward on a garden path, choking, twitching, spitting gravel . . .

Gideon moved to help him but was halted by gasps and screams from behind him. The milkman seemed to have been hit in the arm and was cursing loudly and colorfully. The bus conductor had hurled himself and the librarian to the ground, Mrs. Thomspon was still standing, too petrified with astonishment to move. Harold Neame was dancing with rage, well-mixed, Gideon surmised, with fear.

In fact, thought Gideon in blank despair, they were doing everything *but* obey his orders to back away out of danger. Perhaps from panic, perhaps from an obstinate determination not to desert each other, the fools were staying in the torchlight.

"God help us!" Gideon groaned. "They're asking, begging, *praying* to be killed—"

And no fresh command of his could move them before the gunmen fired again.

There was only one thing he could think of to do.

164

His own revolver in his right hand, a large police torch in his left, he strode forward until he reached the No. 14's garage. The owner of the torch became confused, uncertain whether to play his beam on the advancing Gideon or the huddled patrol. He chose Gideon; and the patrol was plunged back into the relative safety of darkness.

There was an agonizing silence, which was not a silence at all to Gideon; he was nearly deafened by the pounding of his own heart. He could see nothing beyond the beam of the enemy's torch, turned into a dancing blur by the drizzle, which had suddenly become solid rain. He wondered if the rain was the reason why there had been no more shots; it would be driving hard into the attackers' eyes. He did not deceive himself, though. Rain or no, his large frame made him an unmissable target, and the range was point-blank: the garage was less than six feet away.

He stared up unflinchingly into the darkness just above the beam.

Puzzled, for a good two seconds the figures on the roof did nothing; and two seconds was all that Gideon needed.

His own revolver roared once. The bullet whipped into the blackness a fraction to the right of the torch, and plainly hit the hand holding it. There was a startled yelp; the torch went out. At the same instant, Gideon flicked *his* torch on.

"Your turn for a share of the spotlight, lads," he said grimly, and swept its beam up toward the garage roof.

He saw four crouching boys, startlingly youthful. He judged them to be somewhere between thirteen and fifteen years old. Three held revolvers, which were still smoking, or perhaps steaming as a result of the rain. The fourth boy was staring, stunned, at a hand from which blood was dripping. All wore stocking masks but the rain had made the material cling to their faces, and it was possible to see the white, stretched skin beneath; the distorted, but unmistakably frightened eyes; the mouths fallen open with shock, confusion, fear.

"You're right," Gideon said levelly. "This is your comeuppance, you murdering little bastards. Didn't expect it to come quite so soon, did you? Drop those guns, or I'll—"

One of the boys raised his gun, seemed on the point of pressing the trigger. Gideon fired first and caught him in the shoulder. He gasped and swayed. The gun joined the smashed torch on the garage roof.

Then there was a totally unexpected interruption. Gideon heard foot-

165

steps on the pavement, as the cold, donnish voice of Harold Neame cut through the air.

Those stocking-distorted faces did not fool the headmaster for a second. One quick glance upward, and he said, "I know them, Mr. Gideon. I know all of them . . ."

As formally as if he were calling the roll at assembly, he intoned: "Douglas Keating, Roger Wheatland, Clive Matthews, Richard Barratt. Come down this instant, you cowardly, vicious, besotted—killers."

Up till then, the boys had probably hoped that they could somehow shoot or bluff their way out of this situation and escape incognito. At the realization that they were known by name, panic, swept through them. And suddenly—they had gone. There was not a boy in sight. They had all scuttled to the rear of the roof, well out of the torch's range, and the next instant, a series of heavy thuds announced that they were jumping from the roof straight down on to the lawn behind the garage. Gasps of pain accompanied two of the thuds, and Gideon wasn't surprised. A drop of seven feet took some absorbing when one had a bullet in the shoulder or a bloody great hole in one's hand . . .

What were the boys playing at, he wondered. They must have known that the police cars would be here in seconds; that the whole area would be cordoned off. Did they really think that by scrambling through a few fences, they could get clean away?

Or . . . weren't they *planning* to get away?

The thought spun Gideon around as fast as the bullet had spun Stanhope. Belatedly, he remembered whose garage this was; whose lawn the boys were now crossing. And he thought he knew just why they had chosen this particular spot for an ambush.

If everything went wrong, and everything *had* now gone wrong, Gerard Manley Hopkins's home was only the length of a short lawn away. The boys had only to smash their way in there, wave their two remaining guns, and three prize hostages would be theirs for the taking.

A five-year-old child.

A helpless young mother.

And a totally unworldly schoolmaster whom they would probably start by shooting out of hand . . . whom they were very likely *under instructions to kill.*

166

With Neame following hard on his heels, Gideon started running along the pavement toward No. 14. If he could be inside the front door before the boys attempted to break in at the back—

Suddenly, things started happening all around him. Two area cars came screaming up, to halt at the curb and spill uniformed men on to the pavement just ahead.

Behind him, he heard the running footsteps of Riddell's patrol approach from the far end of the street.

Closer behind him, he heard his own patrol shouting.

Ignoring everything, he kept on his way, but the distractions had delayed him—infinitesimally, but fatally.

From the rear of No. 14, slicing through the other sounds and instantly silencing them, came the crash of breaking glass; a shot, and then, in a woman's voice, a single, hysterical shriek.

That would be Charlotte. Did it mean that Hopkins had already been—

Gideon forced himself not to think, only to act.

A second later he was on the step of No. 14, hammering authoritatively on the door, and the LADY SAID, "go tAke A flying Dump."

20

Siege

CHARLOTTE HOPKINS'S SCREAM had been the response of her tortured nerves to a solid three minutes of cumulative terror.

It was hard to believe that it *was* only three minutes since that moment when, preparing a milk drink for Gerard in the kitchen, she had first heard strange noises in the garden. Opening the back door and peering out, she had seen four boys come clambering over the fence and go sneaking across the lawn toward the garage.

Charlotte had called out to her husband. He and she had gone into their dining room, which had a large plate-glass sliding door opening on to the garden. Without turning the light on in the room, they had stood and watched . . . and had had a perfect view of everything that had happened: the shooting at the patrol; the appearance, first, of Gideon, then of Harold Neame at their garage gate; the turning of the tables on the boys, and finally . . .

Finally their view had become a little too perfect. They saw the four boys, two of them lurching and stumbling in pain, the other two brandishing guns, coming straight at them across the lawn; heading, in fact, for this very window.

It was exactly like the climax of a nightmare; and there was something nightmarish, too, about the way she and Gerard just stood there, watching the boys come on. It was as though they had been hypnotized into total paralysis.

With a supreme effort, Charlotte shook herself out of it.

"Quick," she whispered urgently. "If we lock the back door, it'll hold them for a moment. Then if you go around the front and fetch the police, Gideon himself, if possible . . . *Gerard.*"

The sense of nightmare was now overpowering. Gerard hadn't moved and was stubbornly resisting all her efforts to make him do so.

"Don't you realize, darling? I *recognize* these boys. And two of them are hurt . . . in need of help. All I have to do is reason with them—"

"Reason?" Charlotte suddenly saw, with terrible clarity, that the word had no real meaning for Gerard. He had seen the gun flashes and heard the shots and the screams from the road; he must have *known* that the boys were killers. Yet, because these facts conflicted with his theories, he had closed his eyes and ears to them completely. There was no point in arguing; only in acting. Charlotte was slight in build, but desperation gave her strength. She seized Gerard's arm and dragged him a couple of steps toward the doorway. But that was as far as she got before the boys' figures loomed up outside the plate-glass door, their black silhouettes like something out of a horror movie, totally blotting out what little light there was in the room.

The next second came the crash as the glass was kicked in. Despite the fact that two of them were wounded, the boys marched into the room like storm troopers. Charlotte remembered having read somewhere that toward the end of World War II, many of Hitler's storm troopers had been only fifteen . . .

One of the boys fired a shot up at the ceiling. It was intended to frighten; and it succeeded. The crack in that confined space was deafening. Gerard started violently. Charlotte imagined for a moment that he'd been hit, and screamed—a long, piercing, hysterical scream.

The echoes of it had not died away when there was a deafening knocking on the front door.

And the knocking itself was still continuing when there were sounds from upstairs: Karen screaming, "Mummy!" and starting to run out of her bedroom across the landing.

That cured Charlotte of her hysteria in a second. Karen could trip and fall downstairs . . .

170

Forgetting everything except the possible danger to her daughter, Charlotte rushed for the door. But a hand gripped her from behind and a gun was pressed into the back of her neck. It was the gun that had just been fired; the muzzle scorched her flesh.

One of the boys reached the door instead of her and switched on the light in the hall. The knocking on the front door continued; it was even louder now. There were stumbling footsteps on the stairs, and Karen appeared in her nightgown, a curly-haired, freckle-faced little girl whose eyes became wide with horror at the sight of the boy in the stocking mask. She was too frightened to scream; to do anything except give a little moan as he seized her, and pressed a revolver against her head.

"Whoever you are out there," the boy shouted toward the front door, "get this. Unless you are back outside the garden gate by the time I've counted five, there will be a very dead little girl in this family. If you don't believe me, take a squint through the letter box . . ."

And he held Karen so that she, and the gun at her head, was in full view of the front door. Karen moaned softly once again. She was shivering, and her face was almost blue . . .

"Put down that child and wrap something warm around her," roared the voice of George Gideon from the doorstep. "Then let me hear from Mr. Hopkins, so that I can be sure he's still alive. That's the only way you'll persuade me to do as you say."

The boy hesitated; then slowly put Karen down. He took a coat that was hanging on a hook by the front door and wrapped it around her. Then he called at Gerard, with sneering politeness, "Talk to the policeman, will you please, Mr. Hopkins?"

Hopkins came out of the dining room and stood for a moment blinking in the light of the hall.

"Daddy!" Karen said, and ran to him.

"There, there," Hopkins told her. "You mustn't worry, pet. These are quite nice boys, really. They're only playing games." He called out in the direction of the door. "There's no need for you to worry, Mr. Gideon. I am sure these boys mean no real harm. It was very foolish of my wife to scream like that . . ."

Back in the darkness of the dining room, Charlotte felt more helpless than she had ever been in her life. Her neck was still being blistered by the heated muzzle of the gun. The boy who was holding it, excited by her fear,

171

had grabbed her hair with his left hand and was pulling it with cruel strength.

And now she could hear Gideon's footsteps going away down to the front gate, which meant that she was alone with four murderous, sadistic youths, a terrified five-year-old daughter, and a husband who had lost all touch with reality.

She gritted her teeth because she feared that, at any moment, she might be foolish enough to scream again.

WHEN A GRIM-FACED Gideon came out through the front gate of No. 14, he found himself in a crowded street. All four of the area cars had now arrived, in answer to his walkie-talkie summons. An ambulance had arrived, too; Stanhope was being carried into it on a stretcher. The Irish milkman, who had been nicked by a bullet in the arm, was also being attended to by ambulance men, and so was Mrs. Thompson, who seemed to be suffering from shock. The rest of Gideon's patrol had joined up with Riddell's, and they were all waiting beside the gate for his instructions, with Riddell himself at their head. Riddell had already given orders for the uniformed men from the area cars to surround the Hopkins's house.

"We've got six men in the garden," he said briefly. "They're to remain hidden and not to approach within two yards of the house without further orders—unless, of course, there's an escape bid by one of the boys. Was that right, sir?"

"Quite right," Gideon said; and try as he would, he couldn't keep a certain note of bitterness out of his voice. It looked as though Tom had been absolutely right at every stage of the case, and he, Gideon, had been absolutely wrong. Far from stemming the violence, the Gideon's Force project seemed to have escalated it. And he couldn't deny that the civilian patrols *had* faced a risk—a far more serious one than he had envisaged. Only a miracle had saved the six members of his patrol from a massacre.

It was too dark to be sure, but he thought he detected an "I told you so" gleam in Riddell's eyes. He forced himself to admit that it had every right to be there.

Aloud, he said, brusquely. "We're facing a clear siege situation . . . and I needn't tell you what that means."

So many terrorists across Europe had extracted so much from govern-

172

ments by means of sieges that Scotland Yard had made a special study of the subject, and after consultation with the Home Office, Interpol, and a panel of psychiatric experts, had laid down a set pattern of procedure to be followed.

As soon as a siege situation was established, the premises had to be surrounded; after that, there had to be an hour's "cooling-off" period, with the besiegers left alone with their victims. The theory was that human contacts developed that would lessen the risk of violence. The "cooling-off" period also allowed time for special equipment to be brought to the scene: loud speakers for talking to the terrorists, bugging devices for monitoring their whispered conversations with each other, and so on. Special personnel were often brought in at this stage, too; from consultant psychiatrists to engineers with specialized knowledge. It was also not unusual for the case to be taken over by Sir Reginald Scott-Marle in person.

In other words, Gideon thought, he was in all probability about to see one of the trickiest cases of his career taken clean out of his hands.

He had no choice, though, but to implement the set procedure.

He walked up to the nearest area car and used its radio to put himself in direct contact with the Yard. A moment later, he was barking instructions that special siege equipment and personnel should be sent to 14 Naughton Avenue.

As an afterthought, he said, "Is Deputy Commander Hobbs there, by any chance?"

He knew that Alec was working late at the Yard, but it would be a wonder if he was still there as late as this. Luck proved to be on his side. Alec was in his office, and the Yard radio room switched him through.

Gideon briefly outlined the situation and ended, "Someone ought to ring Scott-Marle, give him the facts, and ask him if he wants to intervene personally. Can you handle that?"

"Will do, George. It might take a minute or two to track him down; I've an idea he's attending a dinner somewhere tonight. But I'll get to him as fast as I can. After that, would you like me to come down to the Wellesley Estate myself?"

Gideon was tempted, but then he remembered that Alec had had a heavy enough day of his own.

"That won't be necessary tonight. Tomorrow, perhaps, if this turns out to be a long drawn out affair—and I'm still in charge," he said.

"Do you think it will drag on?" Alec asked.

"I don't see how it can," Gideon said. "Two out of the four boys have bullet wounds badly needing attention. Ordinarily, I'd say that the gang *must* give in—perhaps even before the 'cooling-off' hour's up. But . . ."

He paused for so long that Alec must have thought they'd been cut off.

"But what?" he prompted.

Grimly, Gideon said, "Alec, Tom Riddell has warned me repeatedly not to underestimate the enemy in this case. At last the penny's dropped, and I've realized how right he was. So I'm making no predictions about the outcome. Anything could still happen—including murder."

He switched off the radio and stepped back from the patrol car. The rain was now falling heavily. It matched his spirits, which were heavy with a combination of weariness, anxiety, and a sickening sense of failure. He walked back to the stretch of pavement outside No. 14 where Riddell was talking to Harold Neame.

Riddell was obviously reasserting his favorite theme.

"After months of gruelling inquiries," he was saying, "we are not one inch nearer to knowing who, or what, we're really up against."

From the direction of No. 14 came the sound of Karen crying. Gideon started talking, partly to drown the sound, partly to fight down his frustration at the thought that there was nothing he could do.

"I think I can tell you something about what we're up against," he said. "I believe we're looking for a man who meets the following conditions. *One.* He is an active member of a terrorist group—how else would he be able to obtain and distribute revolvers so easily? *Two.* He is in daily contact with a large number of children, particularly boys between thirteen and fifteen, whom he dominates completely and makes the 'hit men' of his gang. *Three.* He is a well-known resident of the Estate, able to move very freely around it without arousing suspicion. From this it follows—*four*—that he is very clever at hiding his fanaticism from everyone except his schoolboy dupes. We shall probably find that his closest colleagues—even his wife, if he has one—have no idea what he is really like."

Gideon stopped there, surprised himself at how far his musing had taken him. Harold Neame was staring at him owlishly through the rain.

174

"It almost sounds as if you suspected—"

There were suddenly more shrieks from the house. Gideon was on the point of ignoring the "cooling-off" regulations and charging up to the front door, when a uniformed constable came up to him.

"There's a message for you on the radio, sir. Car A4."

Would this be Scott-Marle, wanting to take personal charge?

Gideon walked stiffly to the car—and received one of the biggest surprises of the night. It was the Wellesley substation calling, with the news that Kate had telephoned from the hospital and wanted to speak to him urgently.

"Mrs. Gideon is on the line now, sir. I'll—er—try to connect you," the Wellesley sergeant said. He probably meant that he was going to hold the telephone receiver close to the microphone.

There were a lot of background crackles, and Kate's voice was faint, but her actual words came through plainly enough.

"George," she began with a rush. "I was finally allowed into the intensive care unit here, and I've been with Marjorie and Eric all this time."

"How is Eric? Is he out of the coma?"

"Yes, but he's mostly delirious, and it's hard to catch what he says. But—George." Despite the crackles, there was no mistaking the sudden urgency in Kate's voice. "One thing got through that struck me as being so odd, that I thought you ought to know about it straight away. Don't forget he's delirious, probably doesn't know or mean what he's saying, but—"

Gideon's own voice began to catch Kate's urgency.

"Go ahead, love. Just tell me what the boy said," he told her breathlessly.

"All right." Kate's voice was suddenly loud and clear and unhesitating. "Eric sat bolt upright in bed and screamed, *'I tell you, I couldn't help Gideon coming to my house. You can't let them kill me for it—Mr. Hopkins.'*"

21

Gideon's Force

RIDDELL'S JAW DROPPED when Gideon told him what Kate had said. "*Hopkins?* But that's crazy—"

"Is it, Tom?"

Gideon's face, in the light from the front doorway of No. 14, Hopkins's own home, was almost ferocious with the intensity of his suppressed excitement.

"Think what we know about Hopkins. First—he's form master to Eric Beresford and a lot of the other boys in Eric's gang. Secondly—he was viciously attacked last night by that same gang . . . which rather skillfully managed to slash his suit and shirt to pieces without harming an inch of his skin. Certainly, he was coshed—but a tap would have been enough to make a convincing bruise, and the rest could have been faked. Thirdly—when we try to elicit from him some clues as to the identity of his attackers, he immediately throws a faint."

"Yes, but George," Riddell said. "Eric's knifing took place only about twenty minutes after you and I got to that vigilante meeting. Just before that meeting, we'd left Hopkins at the police station, apparently unconscious. So how could he possibly have been involved in what happened to Eric?"

"Very easily," Gideon said grimly. "We know that he recovered rapidly from his faint and was driven home in a police car within a few minutes. When he got home, he upset his wife by refusing to go to bed. He then apparently went out and started roaming the Estate.

"That could mean that he immediately went to a callbox—one of the few not vandalized—and contacted the headquarters of the gang. Eric, we can take it, was already there—he'd been part of the mob who staged the phoney attack on Hopkins half an hour earlier and was probably still hanging around with the boys. But the boys were already worried about him; the news had come in from one of their spies that I had been seen coming and going from Eric's home.

"When this was reported to Hopkins, he must have realized that his whole operation was in danger. Eric was a policeman's son; his mother was friendly with the head of the CID. Under the combined pressure of his mother and me, the boy might well have broken down and told everything.

"So my guess is that Hopkins had Eric called to the telephone and questioned him. And that as a result of those questions, he gave orders for Eric to be 'taken for a ride,' murdered in fact, and dumped outside his own home."

Harold Neame was so aghast that he could barely speak.

"You're telling me that boys of thirteen, fourteen, fifteen—Eric's schoolmates—tried to kill him in cold blood and then dumped his body *from a car?*"

"They may have got an older boy to drive them," Gideon said. "But I'm afraid they weren't too young to have done the rest. Haven't we just seen four boys in that age-group cold-bloodedly trying to mow down a whole patrol? If they can contemplate that, what's the knifing of an old schoolchum?"

Harold Neame said nothing. He just stared, blankly, despairingly, into the darkness and the streaming rain.

Riddell said, "But all this evidence is highly circumstantial and based on a boy's ravings in delirium . . ."

"So far," Gideon said relentlessly. "But let's take the rest of Gerard Manley Hopkins's known doings last night. Until as late as two A.M., he was out and about on the Estate, visiting boys and their parents. We assumed that he was inquiring into who had attacked him and trying to spread peace and brotherhood. But supposing that was just an act—to make the parents think what an unworldly, forgiving man he was? And supposing his real purpose was something quite different? By that time, the vigilante meeting was long over, and the first Gideon's Force patrols were on the streets. Hopkins could have been observing the routes the patrols took, laying plans to ambush one of the patrols next day, and, under cover of his 'friendly' visits, *actually issuing instructions to the ambushers* . . . Tom!"

Gideon's voice, icily controlled, held the relentless pressure of one about to recognize, to arrest at last, the creeping evil that had held them all in thrall.

"You told me this morning that you had a list of the houses Hopkins was seen visiting. You'd checked with Mr. Neame, you said, and found that a boy from Wellesley High School lived in every one. . . . Do you happen to have that list on you now?"

"If he hasn't, it doesn't matter," Harold Neames said quietly. "I happen to possess a tolerably retentive memory, Mr. Gideon, though I imagine few headmasters would readily forget the names of their boys who were under police suspicion . . . I can guess what it is you want to know, and I can tell you straight away that the answer is in the affirmative. Douglas Keating, Roger Wheatland, Clive Matthews, and Richard Barratt—the charming quartet who are now in No. 14—were the very boys whose homes Hopkins visited last night."

There was a long pause.

"Then that settles it," Riddell breathed.

"It settles it all right," Gideon said grimly. "It also puts rather a strange light on this siege. Hopkins obviously *ordered* the boys to use his garage roof for their ambush. Presumably he wanted to keep a personal eye on such a major operation. And probably he told them that in the very last extremity—if everything went wrong, and they were cornered by the police—they could come into the house and 'capture' him, with his wife and daughter." Karen's screaming had started again; Gideon listened to it now with a dry, humorless smile. "From the sounds they've made and are making, I rather doubt if his wife and daughter are in the plot."

Neame ran a hand through his straggly hair, sodden and bedraggled with the pouring rain.

"We can take it, though, that none of that family are in any real danger."

179

"None," Gideon agreed. "Unless, of course, a gun goes off accidentally, or one of those boys runs amok. Turn a fifteen-year-old into a brutal fanatic, and you could easily have made yourself a Frankenstein monster."

Disturbing sounds were coming from the house now: crashes and bangs and screams in a woman's voice, while Karen's shrieking went on and on.

This "cooling off" period, Gideon decided, was getting altogether out of hand. It was definitely time to take action—and suddenly he knew exactly what action to take.

At that moment, the police constable from car A4 came up and told Gideon that there was another radio message for him.

This time it *was* Scott-Marle. The commissioner was ringing direct from his house, to which he had just returned from a dinner-party. His voice was far from faint, and there was no crackling; he was coming through via the radio room at the Yard, which had equipment for linking telephone calls directly with the transmitter.

Gideon explained what had happened tersely but clearly. He ended "So you see, it's an extraordinary situation . . . and with your permission, I'd like to handle it in an extraordinary way. I want to move in immediately—not with the police, but with a Gideon's Force patrol."

Scott-Marle's voice suddenly sounded cold.

"Gideon's Force again? Look, George, with the best will in the world, I'm not sure I can authorize that."

Gideon knew exactly what Scott-Marle was thinking. He suspected that he, Gideon, wanted to vindicate his concept of a vigilante force by gaining an eleventh-hour glory for it . . . despite the risk to civilian life and limb.

It was an understandable suspicion, even if it did happen to be completely unfounded.

He said, very firmly, "The patrol I was thinking of, sir, will be a rather special one . . ."

Even so, it took a lot of hard argument to get the commissioner to agree.

TEN MINUTES LATER, almost exactly twenty-four hours after Gideon's Force had been born, the last chapter in its short, strange history began.

The "very special" patrol assembled quietly outside No. 14 in the streaming rain.

It consisted of Gideon, Riddell, Harold Neame, half a dozen volunteers from Gideon's and Riddell's patrols—and four brand-new recruits, who had just been rushed from their homes by police car.

They looked pale and shaken, these four, and stood apart from the rest in a strained and silent huddle.

Which wasn't surprising, Gideon thought: they represented the half of the Estate that had been hiding behind a self-made wall of silence through week after week of terror.

They were, respectively, the fathers of Douglas Keating, Roger Wheatland, Clive Matthews, and Richard Barratt.

GIDEON SPOKE TO them as gravely as though they were teenage delinquents.

"The news of the trouble your sons are in may have been a big shock to you. But I doubt if it came as a complete surprise. I suspect that you have all been living for months with the fear that, one day, a summons like this would come. Aren't I right?"

No one spoke, but the very silence indicated assent.

"Now the situation is this," Gideon went on. "There's no blinking at the fact that your sons have tried to carry out a major crime: nothing less than multiple murder. They will have to pay for that, and go on paying for it, probably for the rest of their teens. But not for the rest of their lives, because, thank God, actual murder has not, in fact, been done. And it is because neither you nor I want to see it done that I have brought you here tonight.

"If a normal police raid is carried out on that house, there is a likelihood of shooting. But if *we* all go in, that likelihood, at the sight of you, will be reduced to nil."

"Are you really sure of that?" one father said. It was the most abject admission of parental helplessness that Gideon had ever heard.

"Yes," he answered simply. "The only moment of human feeling the boys have shown so far was when their headmaster, Mr. Neame here, recognized them and called out their names. They stopped being monsters, at that moment, and became frightened schoolboys. I hardly think that the presence of their parents will have less effect.

There was an awkward pause.

181

"But—we'll be arresting our own sons. Or, at least, helping in their arrest," one father said.

"No, you won't. You'll simply be witnessing it," Gideon told him. "All the arresting will be done by Mr. Riddell and me, whether you are there or not. And if the boys make a break for it, I wouldn't expect—or wish—you to try to hold them in any way. There will be a ring of police surrounding the house. Stopping an escape can be left entirely to them. I simply want you there as a reminder to the boys that they're basically human beings, not faceless terrorists. And I really believe that with your cooperation, there will be very little trouble indeed."

"No?" Riddell said suddenly. "Supposing Hopkins has a gun and starts firing?"

For the thousandth time in this case, Gideon wanted to swear at Riddell.

"You and I have guns, Tom," he said sharply. "Between us, we can handle him."

But the damage was done.

The fathers were staring at Gideon with dazed incredulity.

"*Hopkins?*" said one. "You mean he's . . . he's . . ."

Gideon took a deep breath, and then decided to follow his usual policy. When in doubt, confide in the public; tell them the facts straight.

"I have reason to suspect," he said slowly, "that Hopkins is the leader of the gang, the instigator of all that has been happening in this Estate. And that the siege of himself and his family is basically a fake. It's only a suspicion, mind, but there's already evidence to support it—and it's possible that you can give me more. I happen to know that Hopkins visited each of your homes last night. Tell me. Did he at any time talk to your boys *alone*? Do you think he could have been giving them—orders—"

Gideon broke off. From the look on the men's faces, it was clear enough that the answer, in each case, was "Yes."

The father of Douglas Keating was the first to spell it out. Hopkins and his son had been left in the dining room together for more than half an hour. At one point, he had peeped in at the door, and had seen them poring over a diagram or map . . .

"Hopkins was probably showing him the best way to get into his garden and across to the garage roof."

Keating wiped sweat from his forehead. "And I, I was fool enough to

182

think what a wonderful man Hopkins was. He told me he'd forgiven my son for his part in a terrible and vicious attack."

The father of Clive Matthews burst out, "It isn't only you who's been made a fool of, Keating. Hopkins came around to my house quite late last night, well after midnight. Said he wanted to talk to Clive urgently. I got Clive out of bed and then made myself scarce for all of forty minutes while he talked to him in the den. I was so impressed at the thought of a schoolmaster working so late that I actually gave him beer and sandwiches afterward. Made the bastard feel right at home—and went on to argue with him on social problems till nearly two! To think that what he'd really come for was to poison my son's mind—give detailed instructions for him to go out and—and kill—"

The rest of Matthews's words were drowned by one of the oddest and most terrible sounds that Gideon had ever heard. It came from mouths that were dry with horror, throats that were choked by a fury too strong for words, and it emerged as something as deep and menacing as an animal's growl. Yet its meaning was plain enough.

It was the sound of men deciding, with one accord, that another man was not fit to live.

It was the sound of murder.

And suddenly the other members of the patrol were being infected by it, and being less emotionally involved, they were the more articulate.

"Stringing him up to the nearest lamppost's too good for him!" someone cried.

Gideon swallowed hard. He needed no telling what was happening. The two halves of the Wellesley community—those who had always been violently angry and those who, until now, had been cowed—were united at last: united in a rage that was making the very air throb with hate.

The whole object of starting Gideon's Force had been to channel and contain this rage. But what hope was there of channeling or containing it now? Any of these fathers, in this mood, would be fully capable of grabbing a gun from his son, turning it on Hopkins, and emptying it without a moment's thought of the consequences.

He couldn't risk anything like that happening. Wouldn't it be better to abandon the whole idea of using a Gideon's Force patrol and send a police contingent into No. 14 instead?

For just a moment, Gideon hesitated, his brain whirling like a dervish in a crazy dance of doubt. During that moment, something occurred that had very rarely happened to him before. The situation slipped clean out of his control.

As if impelled by a force stronger than themselves, the fathers went ahead of him through the gate of No. 14 and, with the rest of the patrol behind them, began walking up the path to the front door.

"Stop!" Gideon shouted.

They stopped, but not because of the command. A sequence of sounds was coming from the house startling enough to stop anyone.

The little girl, Karen, had started screaming again, the terrible monotony of sound suddenly pierced by an agonizing shriek from Charlotte. The shriek changed to a choking groan of agony and died away. Karen's screams stopped too, as if she was too horrified to go on. There was nothing left but a stunning, chilling silence.

With Riddell behind him, Gideon rushed past the patrol to the front door. Pulling out his revolver, he fired a shot into the lock and then shouldered the door open.

One of the boys—Richard Barratt—was standing at the back of the hall. He had discarded his stocking mask. His face was pale and strained. At the sight of Gideon, he raised his gun. Before he could fire, he caught sight of his father, gasped, and dropped the gun to the floor.

"Where are the others?" Gideon barked.

The boy gestured wildly toward the door of the dining room, which was slightly ajar.

Brushing past him, Gideon reached the door and kicked it wide open.

The light in the dining room was now on, and the scene that it revealed was to stay with Gideon for the rest of his life. It left the patrol, crowding behind him, numbed and motionless.

The two wounded boys—Douglas Keating and Roger Wheatland— were huddled by the shattered window. They had both lost a lot of blood, which bespattered everything near them. They were taking little or no part in the proceedings and were like nothing so much as sick animals cowering in a corner.

A yard or so away from them, half-hidden under a highly polished table, the little girl, Karen, was cowering, too; in her case it was plainly from sheer terror.

She was staring at her mother, who was lying on the carpet, unconscious and perhaps dying. Blood on Charlotte's hair suggested that she had received a severe blow, probably from the butt of a revolver.

The fourth boy—Clive Matthews—was clearly the one who had done the battering. He was standing with his back to a sideboard, with a gun in his hand: Gideon noticed that fresh blood from the butt was staining his fingers. Obviously he had been in charge of Charlotte Hopkins and had overreacted to her final scream of fury.

There was no danger of him overreacting to anything now. The gun was pointing harmlessly at the floor; the bloodstained hand was trembling.

And the cause of all this trembling and cowering was the man who knelt beside the body of his wife, completely oblivious, unaware and indifferent to what was going on; utterly unconcerned as to the fate of the boys who had been his dedicated disciples.

NO ONE WAS in a state to offer resistance or to make any kind of trouble. Hopkins was prostrated by his grief. The boys were paralyzed with shock at having been abandoned by their leader and confronted by their parents, all in the same few seconds. And horror at what had happened, coupled with the sight of their children covered in blood, stanched the fury of the fathers in the patrol and turned it into a kind of dazed, bewildered acceptance.

As a result, the arrests that followed were as quiet and orderly as any Gideon had known.

Which didn't stop the press from loudly proclaiming Gideon's Force as being a triumph for law and order, common sense, and the will of the people . . .

185

22

Penny's Day

THAT WAS VIRTUALLY the end of the Wellesley Estate case, though not of the trail of human tragedy that it had left in its wake.

A doctor and an ambulance were summoned for Charlotte. Hopkins pleaded to be allowed to stay with his wife until they arrived, but Riddell, mindful of the violence that had so narrowly been avoided, would have none of it. Within seconds, he had piled Hopkins and the four boys into police cars, and ordered them to be driven off to the Wellesley substation. It was less than a minute's journey, not too much, he reckoned, for the injured boys to stand. It would be far better to get them away from No. 14 and arrange medical attention for them at the station. Riddell himself went with them. As chief detective superintendent on the case, he was the one who would draw up the official charges.

The fathers also left, looking more wan and lost than their sons and wondering which would be better: to go to the police station and watch their boys being charged and clapped into cells, or to wander mournfully back to their homes and the task of comforting inconsolable wives.

Gideon waited at No. 14 for the arrival of the doctor. His report on Charlotte was fairly hopeful. "Severe concussion, of course," he said. "But nothing broken, no sign of internal hemorrhage . . . I've seen worse cases come through." She was rushed off in the ambulance to Fulton North

General Hospital, where she was put in an intensive care unit—not far, incidentally, from Eric Beresford.

The immediate problem of what to do about Karen was solved swiftly. It turned out that Harold Neame knew the child quite well; Hopkins had on several occasions brought her to the school. Neame's cold, donnish manner held no terror for her, and she went with him willingly, holding fast to his hand with confidence and trust.

"We must take very great care of her," Gideon said, painfully aware of what she had been through. With her father whisked off to the police station and her mother shot off to hospital, the child had been virtually orphaned in seconds; and those seconds had come after an hour of terror that could have scarred her mind for life. Gideon did not like remembering how long he had waited outside the house, listening to Karen's screams and doing nothing—first because of the "cooling-off" regulations and later because he had been waiting to round up the fathers. If only he had followed his heart, and not his mind, and gone into the house earlier . . .

Evidence was soon forthcoming, however, that showed that if he *had* acted more hastily, there would have been a grave risk of gunplay. Two revolvers were found on Hopkins when he was searched at the station, and a hoard of twenty more came to light at the back of the attic of No. 14, together with fifty rounds of ammunition.

Next day, the police made more discoveries at No. 14. A bureau desk in the front room was found to have a secret drawer, packed with papers identifying Hopkins as one of the leaders of "Youth Against Society," a secret organization aiming at, as one badly printed pamphlet put it, "incessant guerrilla warfare in every urban center, carried out by our heroic young." The pamphlet continued: "Great care should be taken to conceal the political reasons for our activities. They should appear to be simply criminal actions carried out by a mindless mob. Thus our real purpose will never be suspected until total victory—the complete breakdown of law and order throughout society—has been achieved." Other pamphlets showed how the children were to be caught at an early age, indoctrinated with the belief that violence and heroism were identical virtues, and systematically trained to be tough and ruthless killers.

Gideon passed all these documents on to Special Branch, who were delighted to receive them; they provided confirmation of a great deal that

188

had been suspected, but never proved. The work of identifying and routing out Hopkins's confreres in a dozen different areas was intensified. Gideon felt that he owed Special Branch a favor after their help with the Dino Orsini affair. He was glad that the chance to repay the debt had come so soon.

Further details of the "Youth Against Society" operations in Wellesley gradually came to light after Hopkins's arrest. Horrified at the thought of the massacre that had so nearly taken place, more and more families in the Estate broke their silence. In addition, Eric Beresford provided vital information under several different headings. He described the knifing in the car in detail, but refused to name the boy who had wielded the knife. *He* would have knifed someone equally readily, he said, if Hopkins had ordered him to do so. "Wouldn't have thought anything of it," he added. It was clear that after conducting a successful summer-long reign of terror, the gang had been punch-drunk on violence—and on the heady belief that they could get away with anything.

Putting Eric's testimony and that of other witnesses together, a picture began to emerge of how the organization had been run. Eric, and about twenty other boys, used to meet Hopkins once a week after school-hours—usually in the basement of a disused riverside warehouse on the outskirts of the Estate. These boys, all aged between thirteen and fifteen, became almost worshipers of Hopkins and formed the hard-core membership of the gang. Sometimes older teenagers were roped in, but only for special duties, such as driving getaway cars or attempting to break up the vigilante meeting. These older boys also helped to create the Estate-wide spy network, but there their involvement ended. They were never allowed to attend the warehouse sessions, and it was around these that everything had really revolved.

Here the younger boys had received their orders for all their major activities—the organized rampages of vandalism, the fire-raising, the muggings. But the gang also had an operational headquarters nearer the center of the Estate; one of the boys, whose parents were out until late every evening, had offered the use of his home—and telephone. It was here that Eric had been seized by his fellow gang-members, when Hopkins had ordered his killing.

Most of the training of the boys—the actual process of turning them into "urban guerrillas"—had been done in the warehouse basement, a room that had been sound proofed by the judicious use of sandbags. The program had ranged from target practice with revolvers to "nothing-barred" fights, using razors, chains, and flick knives.

In one of the flick knife fights, Eric had stabbed his opponent in the shoulder, his own shirt being smeared with his victim's blood. It was this incident that had led to Marjorie calling in the Gideons for help.

Because Eric had subsequently suffered so much—largely as a result of his, Gideon's, rashness in visiting his home so openly—Gideon decided to ask Riddell not to press charges against him.

Marjorie must have guessed what had happened. On the day that Eric was released from hospital, he and his mother came around to Gideon's home to thank him.

Marjorie Beresford's face was alight with gratitude. "If there's anything I can ever do for you, Mr. Gideon . . ."

Gideon grinned.

"Aren't you forgetting? My daughter's getting married in two weeks' time. We're relying on *you* to see that she doesn't turn up at St. Margaret's in rags and tatters . . ."

THE WEDDING OF Alec Hobbs and Penny Gideon was one of the most notable occasions of the London social year. It was also one of the most extraordinary. When before in history had there assembled a congregation containing both the commissioner of the metropolitan police and the conductor of the BBC Symphony Orchestra, surrounded by pews full of the nation's leading policemen—and its finest musicmakers?

All of the Yard's top men turned up. Riddell, looking more relaxed than Gideon had seen him for weeks; Lemaitre, grinning as irrepressibly as ever; Matt, smiling, as if without a care in the world.

Penny, serenely aware of the greatness of the occasion, looked breath-taking in a gown of ivory satin and a gossamer veil, which would not have flowed with half so much elegance if Marjorie Beresford had not worked on it with such inspired skill.

Kate was magnificent too, though there were moments when her hand crept out to Gideon's for comfort, as the tears filled those deceptively calm gray eyes. Penny was the last of their children to be leaving home. The gap in their lives caused by her departure would take some filling. Perhaps would never be completely filled.

It was shortly after the ceremony when there came, for Gideon, the most memorable moment of this most memorable of days.

He and Kate were waiting outside the church for the car to take them to the reception, when an old man stepped suddenly out of the crowd of sightseers that were gathered at the gates.

"I hope you will pardon this intrusion, Mr. Gideon, but I have for some time felt a desire to meet you, and this seemed a fitting opportunity."

Puzzled, Gideon looked at him without recognition. "I'm afraid this is no occasion for meeting *me*," he said gently. "It's my daughter Penny's day."

The old man smiled gravely.

"Ah. Your daughter. Concerning her, I have the best of news. All the indications are that she will have much love, much happiness in the days ahead—she and her husband too."

The old man smiled, bowed, and stepped back into the crowd, leaving Gideon with nothing but the memory of two deep-set, haunting eyes.

"Obviously a nutcase," he muttered to Kate.

Kate smiled. "Perhaps—but he sounded as though he really knew what he was talking about."

Matt Honiwell, who was standing just behind them, nodded sagely.

"Seeing that that was Jacob Brodnik, George," he said, "I think you can take it that he did."